Vault Diary 01

Hypothesis Oblivion

Dedication

For Staci, Isabella, Sofia, and LaReina
my sky and stars.

Let our adventure begin.

Table of Contents

The Fractured Ledger

Preface - The Fractured Ledger

A.T. 310 Month 2, Day 70 (Galactic Standard Time)
September 5, 2050 (Earth Local Time)

I never intended for these entries to be read.

These aren't meant for history. They are not part of the *Book of Maze.* I wrote them in quiet moments between disasters — in notebooks, on datapads, on anything I could find. They are the source materials. Mine. When I could write, I did. When I couldn't, I remembered. I captured what I could when there was time for pen to meet paper.

I gave those memories to Terowe. He was the one who asked me to preserve them. At first, I told him no. He wanted to shape them into stories. He said there were those in your world who would see value in my prattling. What do I have to lose? Nothing, I guess.

I agreed, with a few conditions: the entries had to stay in the order I wrote them. Anything else would've been dishonest. Terowe pushed back at first, but we came to an agreement. He gave the stories and entries names. He asked me one question about each story and curated my reply into an introduction, sticking only to my words. In exchange, he left the diary entries themselves untouched.

He wanted to include them in the *Book of Maze.* I didn't want my personal feelings to become part of my family's history book.

Vault Diary - Hypothesis Oblivion

The *Book of Maze* is about my House, my people. Its creation is my duty: to preserve, for posterity, our place in time. My personal grief, my choices, my failures... they feel small compared to that. I don't believe they deserve the same binding. *The Vault Diaries* are our compromise.

Our final disagreement was where the stories should begin. Terowe listened to me on this one, so forgive me if this doesn't flow as you might expect. I chose the point that I see as my origin, the place where I think my life truly began. No disrespect to my mother. I think she'd understand.

What you are about to read is not a novel. It's the reality of me.

-Maria Zadak Maze

P.S. A Brief Note on Conversions and Time

Earth exists in what we call the Conduit Universe, a separate dimension from mine, though not all that different in spirit. I did not allow Terowe to change my journals for the most part, but I did convert most of my world's metrics and terms into your equivalents. Some words, however, have no translation.

For example, you measure a year based on your planet's orbit around the sun, even though the other planets in your system take wildly different amounts of time. I suppose when you're a species bound to a single world, it makes sense to base your time system on your own rotation and orbit.

Thankfully, we outgrew that.

The Fractured Ledger

In the Kameonic Universe, we have a Standard Year, a shared system that keeps every planet aligned. Each world may have its own climate and seasonal chart based on its orbit, but the year is the same length everywhere. Our Standard Year is about 25% longer than yours, divided into fifteen months, which makes each month roughly comparable to one of yours.

Day and night are still local, of course. The number of days per month and hours per day vary depending on where you are. Don't worry, I've included the Planetary Time Conversion Chart we use, with an extra entry for Earth using our time scale, so you can follow along without doing the math.

You're welcome.

Planetary Time Conversion Chart

Planet/Environment	Hours/Day	Days/Month
Galactic Standard Time	11	100
Tula	20	53
Voltaire III	30	35
Foretto	43	25
Alphaeus	18	60
Earth	34	31

Story 01: Alejandro Jabez

Before him, there was order. Not peace. Not happiness. A rhythm I understood. School. Home. My attic. Books stacked to the ceiling, projects half-finished. Silence and solitude, my loyal servants. My mother was the center, overbearing and predictable. Even grief and loneliness had their rules. I was eleven. I accepted that people didn't understand me. I didn't expect them to. I had her, the woman I called Mother, my overlord. I didn't love the way she shaped my life, but I made peace with it.

Then came the storm.

Vault Diary - Hypothesis Oblivion

Diary Entry # 01 – Unwanted Arrival

A.T. 268, Month 14, Day 26 (Tulan Standard Time)

I'm always excited to see Aunt Linda. Why wouldn't I be? She's the best "aunt" a girl could ask for. Always brings presents, cooks like a galaxy-class chef, always listens but keeps just the right distance from your business.

Today, for the first time, I was nervous. Not because of her, but because of him—her son.

Mom's been telling me about Alejandro for years. A trouble-maker. A fighter. A problem in need of solving. She never said those words exactly, but I've learned to read between the lines.

She's the one who paid for his alternative schooling after he got kicked out of traditional school, and Centrum Universal Boarding School—basically a penal colony with a faculty. I thought he'd just keep bouncing from place to place, always someone else's problem.

I never thought I'd meet him, especially not today.

Mom told me to "take care of him," like he was family. He's not my family. No obligation. No responsibility. I wouldn't want this as a pet. Still, I tried.

I showed him the forest. He barely spoke, just stomped through the grass with his arms folded, like the natural world offended him.

I showed him my lab in the attic. That's when he decided he had opinions.

"Wow. What a wreck," he said. "How do you find anything?"

"It's a functional system," I said.

He scoffed, actually laughed, and tossed off some joke I didn't bother to catch. I told him to get out. He didn't move until I shoved him. I think he might have been surprised, like he thought I wasn't serious.

He gave the most condescending apology I've ever heard before throwing my lab door open to walk out. He's staying with us for at least a month. I don't know if I can last that long. I might have to arrange an accident to hasten his departure.

Oh, Mom tucked me in and dropped the worst part: he's in my class. Two years older, tall enough to look down at me, strong enough to tackle an ox. Somehow, he's in my class.

Probably just another Stroud. Another bully in different packaging. At least he didn't call me a Mib or accuse me of stealing thoughts. It's hard enough being one of only five Aquians on Tula without my bullies snoring in my ear.

Maybe he'll just be quiet. I hope so.

At least I have something else to think about. Dad's coming home in a few weeks. I can't wait. I don't even know what I'm excited for. He's coming on assignment, not on leave. It's just work disguised as family time.

Mom got him to promise he'd take me to the space observatory while he's stationed here. That's something. Maybe I can steal him from the army for a few hours.

A girl can dream.

Diary Entry # 02 – Unneeded Defenses

A.T. 268, Month 14, Day 27 (Tulan Standard Time)

I'm already tired of writing about my most obnoxious houseguest.

I wouldn't even bother, but something strange happened today. I'll get to that, but first, important things.

My tower model parts finally arrived. Mom was waiting in my room with the boxes when I woke up. She looked thrilled, then immediately told me to move them off the main floor. I was about to haul them upstairs, but the pest beat me to it. Didn't say a word. Just picked them up like they weighed nothing and carried them up to my lab.

I left it alone at first. Got ready for school. No point stopping a good thing. Went up to open the boxes right before breakfast, and he was still up there rearranging my workbench. Said I should be thanking him.

I kicked him out. Again.

At least Aunt Linda's breakfast bowl made up for it. That, and she actually did bring me a book. She just didn't want me too distracted to properly welcome Alley. (That sounds like Mom's idea.)

Oh, and apparently he prefers "Alley." Mom refuses to call him that, which drives him insane. I only write it here to save my hands the extra letters.

Vault Diary - Hypothesis Oblivion

Mom mentioned that Dad's assignment is related to Dark Space, the dense, nebulous cluster just outside our moon where smugglers and assassins hide. I spent most of the day at school trying to find information on it. The textbooks barely mention it. I'll have to find some better sources. If I can help him wrap things up early, maybe that's extra time together.

Speaking of school, Alley got kicked out of class today. I should be writing an "I told you so," complete with a letter begging Mom to send him somewhere else, but...

It wasn't what I thought.

Alley sat right next to me. That was strange all by itself. Nobody ever sits near me. Too dangerous. I'm Aquian. One wrong touch and I might see their darkest secrets.

I mean, I know that's nonsense. I'm only half Aquian, years away from my neurostatic receptors activating. I have to remind Mom every time she tries to force me to wear those stupid antistatic gloves.

Anyway, Stroud spent the whole morning calling Alley "stupid." No response. "Slow." Brushed it off. He called me a Mib three times. Alley ignored it, and so did I. Invade his mind? Yeah, no thanks.

When Stroud called me out the fourth time, Alley snapped. He called the teacher out for not doing anything.

Mrs. Fetchvane tried to deflect the blame, but Alley wasn't having it. I tried to get him to stop. He just got louder. He told her Stroud was mistreating me, and that she was letting him get away with it. He called her a coward.

She kicked Alley out.

The weirdest part? When I got home, he stopped me. Asked if I was okay. Apologized for Stroud's attitude. Offered to take care of him. Said Stroud didn't speak for all Kameonics.

At first, I thought he was hitting on me. I told him I wasn't interested.

His response? "Don't make me vomit."

Then he called me a spoiled brat and said that didn't mean punks like Stroud should treat me that way.

Still processing that.

I need this whole situation to be over. I don't know what to make of this guy.

Mom's only advice? "Stay out of trouble and keep your distance." How does she not see how impossible she made that?

One thing about him does make sense. Stroud's a jerk, but he's not wrong. Alley is terrible at math. If he ever had to multiply a fraction and a number, his brain might actually explode.

Vault Diary - Hypothesis Oblivion

Diary Entry # 03 – Unwelcome Lessons

A.T. 268, Month 14, Day 29 (Tulan Standard Time)

I said I was tired of writing about him. I meant it.

Something happened today, though. Something unexpected.

Before I get to that, my tower model is finally coming together. That's why I didn't write yesterday. By the time I properly anchored the foundation and finished carving the base, I could barely hold a blade, let alone a pen. The foundation is set, and I've started construction. If I keep this pace, it should be done in time for the competition.

Honestly, I would've made more progress, but watching Alley do math is like watching a puppy take the wrong street home while his owner searches for him with a map.

It started at school yesterday. He had an assignment, and I swear he must have swapped brains with a lizard. Numbers in places they didn't belong. Entire equations missing crucial steps. I couldn't stand it. I took his paper, tore it up, and rewrote it with clear explanations. Did half of it for him, too.

He didn't react. No arguing. No whining. No "How dare you touch my work." Just an "okay."

Then he spent the next hour reading my explanation like he was deciphering a lost ancient language.

I thought that would be the end of it.

I saw him at lunch later. I was almost finished finalizing my tower design drawing when he walked up. Left his weird dancing, whatever that was, just to ask me about number seven.

I didn't want to stop. No telling if explaining the question would take ten minutes or two hours, given his first attempt. Trying to avoid another conversation, I told him I'd help after school in my lab, but only if he promised not to clean anything. He said he would.

He lied.

Still, I taught him. I have to admit, he's a good student. Listens. Doesn't argue. Processes information like a machine. He was clearly taught wrong. Not that he couldn't understand; his teachers were just idiots. Some of what they taught was so bad I almost wonder if it was a joke.

He only cleaned my tool chest, and I won't lie, finding my fuses in seconds instead of minutes was nice. Not that I'll ever tell him that.

He also said he'd try to get me a good source on Dark Space. I think he was serious. Not sure if he's bluffing or if he actually knows something. Part of me wants to see if he follows through. I don't know what made me tell him about Dad. He can actually be pretty disarming when he wants to be. Barf. Did I just say that?

Mom is getting herself dolled up for Dad's return, which is ridiculous, because she already wears a ball gown, a red fedora, and white gloves to work with children. How much more put together can she get?

That said, I do like how excited she gets. I like how much they love each other. It's not something I'd ever want for myself, but I won't pretend I don't like seeing it.

She makes every one of his homecomings feel like an event.

Maybe that's half the reason I look forward to him coming home.

That's a lie. I won't correct myself.

Diary Entry # 04 – Forced Productivity

A.T. 268, Month 14, Day 35 (Tulan Standard Time)

I should've known today would be a disaster the moment I opened my eyes. I wanted a weekend. Instead, I got Alley. Two full days of peace, gone. Just him, still here. Still in my space. Still existing.

Alley, the gift that keeps on giving. I swear, I can't roll my eyes hard enough without risking permanent brain damage. I stand by what I said last time: he's not so bad, which somehow makes it worse. I want my time back, and I can't have it. Apparently, my entire weekend now belongs to playing host. And since he's actually kind-hearted and considerate, I can't even take it out on him.

Mom, if you ever read this, know that I will *never* forgive you for this. My me-time is sacred. It's the only thing keeping me sane, and you know why. You're my mother.

Today? Instead of my usual weekend routine, I had to take Alley to the woods so he could train. Which, to be fair, was better than watching him destroy my lab. Yesterday, he cracked my tower. I almost cracked *him.* (Who am I kidding? He'd end me in two shots. Probably one. Maybe he'd just hold me still until I wore out. I think hurting me is beneath him.)

To be fair, he felt terrible and insisted on staying overnight to help me fix it. I know he hated every second of it.

Oh no. I'm getting to know him. Not admitting that.

At least I got some reading done while we were out there. Credit where it's due, Alley actually came through. When I asked him for a good source on Dark Space, I wasn't expecting much. Maybe a smuggler's handbook with half the pages missing. Instead, I got archives, private logs, even declassified reports. More than I could read in a lifetime. How did he get his hands on all this stuff? I'm convinced three of the reports were illegal to possess. He must have a hacker friend somewhere.

I've been devouring it, a separate book read in each ear, another book open in front of me. I'm stuffing my datapad with notes faster than it can compile. I even started a Master Document just to keep track of everything. It might be useless in the end, depending on what Dad's working on, but at least now I have a chance. I could never have done this without Alley. I hate that I know that. Alley didn't say much. Didn't gloat. Just listened, or pretended to.

The only time he broke his silence was when I pointed out the mistake he kept making. There's this kick he was supposed to land, and he just... didn't. Same mistake, over and over again. I watched him for a while before finally asking what he was doing wrong. He showed me a video of how it's supposed to look. I compared it to what he was actually doing, saw the difference immediately, and explained it to him. He stared at me like I had just predicted the future. Asked me how I knew, like the laws of physics aren't universal.

Here's the worst part. The part I'm ashamed to admit. As we were talking, I came up with an idea for a training device, a way to force him to stop making the mistake. I couldn't let go of it. After he went to sleep last night, I started building it. I snuck back into the lab after Mom called lights out. I fell asleep twice trying to measure the material binding. Why couldn't I sleep? I was wrecked. I wanted to quit. I had at least earned a break. I tried, but every time I shut the lab light off, I thought about what he'd found on Dark Space. I heard him muttering, frustrated, beating himself up. I told myself, one more hour.

By 2 a.m., it was done.

I wanted to see if it would work, to be there when he tried it out. No such luck. I left it outside the guest room where he kept his equipment and hid his actual equipment so he'd have to find it. When I finished that little heist, my body took what I'd denied it all those hours. I sat on the stairs just outside the guest room. That's the last thing I remember from my first night of invention.

I woke up in my bed at 9:27 a.m., with him sitting beside me. Not standing. Not hovering. Sitting. Waiting. He just said thank you.

I don't get thanked. I'm not sure I like it. It made everything weird. I just retreated. Looked at my desk, my books, the floor. Anywhere but him. It took me way too long, but I finally muttered, "You're welcome." It didn't come out right. Didn't sound like me. I hated how awkward it felt.

Before I could recover, he asked me to make an adjustment. Showed me what needed fixing. He was right. I adjusted it.

He's been married to that thing ever since. Hasn't missed a single kick. Not once.

Meanwhile, I'm spending today working on my tower. No more distractions. Well, except helping Mom with the planting. I have to do seven hours, and I'm starting late. This is what I get for being helpful.

Diary Update:

I only had to do two hours. Alley took my other five. I don't know what kind of deal he made with Mom, but she came up to me and said it was "handled." I barely had time to process that before he punched me in the shoulder on his way out. Not hard, just enough to make a point.

It hurt more than he realized.

I don't know what made me do it, but when he came back inside, I punched him just as hard. I told him, "My hours are my responsibility. They're how I pay for my things."

He smirked, promised he had no desire to be a farmhand, and apologized for hitting me too hard. Then, before I could even process that, he rubbed his arm. Said my follow-through was off. Offered me a lesson. Apparently, I punch like a toddler. Inaccurate. A toddler flails. I aimed. Just not effectively. Besides, how could it be effective? Alley's about 73% muscle. It's like trying to break a rock with a finger.

I scowled. He laughed.

I got two extra hours of sleep and built the tower's base. Not a wasted day.

I have to get this guy out of my life. I am starting to enjoy having him around.

Diary Entry # 05 – Strategic Silence

A.T. 268, Month 14, Day 42 (Tulan Standard Time)

One day, I'll write a single entry without mentioning Alley. Or maybe I won't. Maybe that wouldn't be a bad thing.

Today was, how do I put this, an absolute disaster.

I've never been a big fan of being Aquian. Sure, perfect memory has its advantages. I'll be able to transmit thoughts when I get older, take thoughts maybe when I'm much older (not that I ever would). I'd trade it all in a heartbeat if it meant not being treated like an existential threat everywhere I go. Or garbage. Or both, which is more common. I didn't ask to be born this way. I hate that people look at me like I'm plotting to steal their soul.

Anyway, this morning everything was fine. Aunt Linda made her corn potato mash with seasoned eggs and goat cheese. I swear, when she dies, God is throwing a welcome-back party. He's been missing his head chef since the day she was born. Every time she leaves for more than a week, I want to kidnap her just for the food.

Spontaneity is a good thing, Mom. Take notes.

School, on the other hand, was terrible.

Stroud started with me in Physical Science. His math was wrong, rare because he's usually almost as good as I am. I pointed out his mistake. He tried to justify it. I could literally pinpoint the exact moment he realized his mistake, but he didn't back down.

Made some joke about me being "too old" and missing a step. Because, you know, gray hair at eleven. Since birth, actually.

(Seriously, we're going to have a discussion about that one too, God. What was the big idea with that?)

Anyway, I broke down the error in his work, said nothing about him, but he still lost it. Mr. Vincent sent him to see Mom, which should have been the end of it. Usually he comes back better, calmer, more controlled. I swear sometimes I think Mom likes Stroud more than me. He always leaves her office with a pocketful of candy and the biggest smile.

Not this time. I guess she was out.

Stroud found me in the hallway alone. That was my first mistake. Never be alone around Stroud when he's having a bad day. He shoved me into a wall. No, slammed me is more like it. My shoulder still hurts. My back is a patchwork quilt of black and blue. He got in my face and told me to "watch myself."

I said if he wanted to hurt me, he'd better get to it. That he didn't scare me. I lied. Still, better than the alternative. I will not be his doormat, no matter how many blows that costs me.

He swung at me, hard. Alley stepped in and caught his wrist. Not blocked. Not deflected. Caught. Like he was intercepting a handshake.

There wasn't even tension in Alley's arm. Still, when Stroud tried to pull away, something in his face changed. Like a flicker of pain or confusion.

He yanked free eventually, but I saw it. That hurt him.

Alley smiled, stepped up to Stroud with an intensity I'd never seen, and said something I didn't catch, just below a whisper. Stroud clearly understood. His expression changed. I couldn't quite place it. Fear, anger, surprise—maybe a mix of the three.

What I did hear him say clearly, he said a decibel louder: "Are we clear? Stay away from my girl."

(I'm his girl now? Hard no.)

Stroud squared up. Swung twice, fast and angry. The first missed, but the second shouldn't have.

Right before it landed, everything in his body just stopped. Like a switch had been flipped. Like whatever message his brain sent never reached his limbs.

He stood there, fist raised, eyes locked, and couldn't finish the motion.

Alley just waited. He put his hands behind his back, watching, smiling wide.

"Finish," he said. "Follow through. You're almost there."

Stroud didn't. Couldn't. When he finally stepped back, he was limping.

Alley didn't say a word to me. I should have asked him something. Demanded an explanation. What was I supposed to say?

"Hey, how did you break him?"

The first punch, he did some kind of quick, fancy block, no counter. Beyond that, I never saw him make contact.

I didn't see Alley again until late tonight. Aunt Linda was chewing him out in the kitchen, something about getting disqualified from a tournament in a few days. She said if he got caught fighting, he could lose his place.

Alley insisted he hadn't done anything to Stroud. "He swung at me. I didn't even defend myself." The strange thing is, I knew he was lying, and yet everything I saw backed him up. He said if they were worried about Stroud, they should take him to a doctor.

Maybe they should. I know what I saw. Stroud was fine before. Couldn't walk after.

"Ask Maria. She was there. Saw the whole thing." His fake innocence slipped into full condescension mode. He winked at me as he walked away. "You know what you saw. Tell her." He smirked when he said it and didn't even try to hide how much he enjoyed the whole thing.

Aunt Linda asked, and I confirmed. As far as I know, that's all I saw.

Later, I asked him about the "my girl" comment. He reminded me that I was "vomit-worthy." Which, so is he. I let him know I don't ever plan on being with anyone, ever, but I also don't want people thinking we're together.

He shrugged and said it was just for Stroud, that he'd step aside if a worthy man came for me.

(I hate how that phrasing bothered me. I don't even know why.)

He assured me I wasn't his type. Then, like it was nothing, he admitted I checked most of his boxes.

I don't know why that made me punch him, but he smirked about it.

I asked him what he did to Stroud. He didn't answer. Just laughed, like it was all a joke, but had this look like he was trying to decide how much to say.

"When you're ready." Then he walked away like it didn't mean anything. It almost felt like a threat. Almost.

Diary Entry # 06 – Edge of the Ring

A.T. 268, Month 14, Day 54 (Alphaeus Standard Time)

I said I'd write one entry without mentioning Alley. Two whole days. That's how long I lasted.

Considering that progress is… concerning. Even worse, I only avoided writing about him because I was buried in tower work and building his training machine.

So, yeah. He's still here, but those two days were about work. Prove me wrong.

We arrived on Alphaeus for the Third Outer Rim Division of the Mast Tournament, the qualifiers. Alley's been training for months and talking about it for weeks.

I wasn't even supposed to come. First, I was staying home. Then, I was just staying in the hotel. Next thing I knew, I was wedged between three screaming six-year-olds and their overwhelmed mother on the train to the arena.

Triplets.

That's why I'm glad I'm barren. Mom calls it a curse; I call it foresight. I'm convinced whatever runs the universe knew I couldn't handle kids and did me a favor. I have enough classmates screwed up by parents who weren't ready but had them anyway. The Maze family may die with me, but I already promised Mom I would write a full family history beforehand. Technically my job anyway, and I hope that's good enough for her. It's all she gets.

Vault Diary - Hypothesis Oblivion

The train dropped us off late. We almost missed Alley's first match. Didn't really care. Too busy trying not to throw up between the smell and the shouting. I'm convinced the fog of musty cheese and chaos could be weaponized. I should ask Dad about that.

Alley is a different person in the ring. He reminds me of my mother: formality, precision, control. Absolutely lethal.

When he landed his first kick, I thought he killed the kid. He didn't, obviously, but the fighter forfeited on the spot. I don't blame him. It was one of the only times Alley broke character; he nearly missed his next fight making sure the boy was okay. A medic pressed regent-serum gauze to the kid's chest, and a few minutes later he was walking again—barely.

Alley fought his way to the finals. His last opponent, another Tulan named Lorenz-I. Fast. Brutal. The first round had a few close calls.

Round two was when Lorenz-I made his move.

I heard the bone crunch from the stands—Alley's arm. His shout hit my soul. Was it over? The wince of pain lasted only a moment before controlled rage took over.

He broke free and gave Lorenz-I a hard kick to the ribs. Alley forced his body back to ready, but he couldn't hold a stance. He could barely lift his right arm.

I don't know what got into me. I moved before I thought, ran toward the stage. Officials stopped me just before the edge.

He kept fighting, one-handed, until they called a break. Lorenz-I actually called it.

I thought I embarrassed him. He had that same furious scowl on his face as he walked over but didn't say a word. When they asked who would set his arm, he looked at me. Gestured for me to come into the ring.

Said I was his coach. Coach!?

I wanted to tell them the truth, that I was just the girl he dragged along. Come to think of it, he was the only fighter there without a coach.

He knelt in front of me, arm limp, waiting. Like he expected me to fix it. I knew what to do. And I did. Thank you, Army field medic training, and the ten hours I spent pretending I wasn't paying attention. I can't be mad at Dad anymore for making me re-certify every year.

He let out one shout, one guttural sound, then said, "Thanks," like I'd handed him a tissue.

Then, for the first time since the tournament started, he gave me that cocky smirk I'm strangely getting used to, like he was saying, *watch me work.*

He stood and went back to the ring like it hadn't happened.

Aunt Linda tried to stop the fight, called for him to quit. He didn't even look at her. Told me later his dad wouldn't stand for a quitter. He got back into his ready position.

Round three, Alley played it safe at first. Lorenz-I pressed hard. I thought it was over. Then I saw it: a shift in his stance, a transfer of weight and balance.

Lorenz-I dodged the first two kicks, unaware. Alley was ready for that. It was the third kick that mattered, and he nailed it. Lorenz-I flew out of the ring. Third ring-out. The crowd erupted in applause.

Match over. It was a good thing too. He fell to a knee three seconds after contact, but who cares!?

Alley won. He really did it.

I screamed—a prissy, high-pitched "I'm shouting for my boyfriend" scream. In front of Mom. Aunt Linda. Alley. An entire stadium full of people. I wanted to melt into the floor. The scream was bad enough, but worse, I screamed because I needed him to win. What do I even do with that?

Mom just stared. Aunt Linda laughed.

Alley didn't say a word. He limped over and pulled me onto the stage. Raised my hand like I was part of the win. Like I belonged up there.

I played along. What else could I do? He received the trophy for winning the Third Outer Rim Division of the Mast Tournament. Alley knelt to his mom, then wrapped his arms around me. I was glowing and proud until that very moment. Wet, sweaty, and gross. That pulled me out of it for a solid five minutes, which I think he enjoyed more than anything else. He had the biggest smile on his face when I pulled away. That boy.

Afterward, he introduced me to Lorenz-I. The guy was all respect, just like Alley. Five minutes ago, they were trying to kill each other. Now they're best friends. Fighters are weird.

We were back home by nightfall. I'm in the lab now. I have to finish this tower. My submission is due in a week.

Diary Update:

Fell asleep in the lab.

I woke up in my bed. Alley was asleep in the chair, bandaged like a busted pipe, regent-serum gauze on his shoulder.

Did he drag me downstairs with one arm? Or maybe Mom helped. Either way, it's official. This boy is crazy.

Then I remembered—I hadn't secured my model.

I ran up to the lab. Already done.

Model secured. Lab spotless. Tools catalogued. How did he do all this with one working arm?

He left a note on my table:

> *Hire a maid. Your mom makes enough.*
>
> *P.S. Close your diary next time. Don't worry. I didn't*
>
> *read it.*

Jerk!

What scares me? I believe him.

I don't know what he is, but he's not just some bruiser with a temper. I'm starting to dread the idea of them moving, of only seeing Alley at school.

What has he done to me?

Diary Entry # 07 – Mib

A.T. 268, Month 14, Day 53 (Tulan Standard Time)

It happened today. My first transmission. I really am a Mib.

I thought I'd be older. Most Aquians transmit their first thought at eight. As a half-breed, I figured I had more time. One doctor even said it might never happen. Guess he was wrong.

The day started like the others, or at least how they've been lately: the best breakfast ever made. Aunt Linda always outdoes herself. They finalized their home purchase, so they're packing to move. It's only been three weeks, but it feels like a lifetime.

I don't want her to go. Not for the cooking, though I will miss that. Back to eggs, rice, beans, and the occasional brick of milled bread (ugh), but that's not why.

I'll miss Alley. Ugh. There, I said it. School's great, but him not being home when I get there, it's not the same.

Speaking of school, Stroud stirred things up again today. This time, over Sarah. Can he just make up his mind already? He and Sarah keep getting together and breaking up. I know every time they do because he starts hovering around lunchtime like a mosquito. Won't leave me alone. If he wasn't such a prick, I'd swear he had a crush on me. Maybe he just wants attention.

Vault Diary - Hypothesis Oblivion

Apparently, she has a thing for Alley right now. He ignores her completely, but since he's still recovering from the tournament, it's harder for him to disappear when she shows up. Turns out he didn't just dislocate his shoulder; he cracked a rib too. Watching Alley squirm every time she brushed against him was entertaining for a while, but...

I'm ashamed to admit this, but I played along with the "his girl" thing. Just long enough to get Sarah to back off. It worked. She stopped hovering. The gossip has already begun, but whatever. It bought him some peace, at least until he can move fast enough to dodge the attention on his own. It would be fun to act out a breakup.

Stroud cornered Alley at recess. Accused him of messing with "his girl." Then shoved his bad shoulder. I saw how much it hurt. He didn't say anything, but I could see it.

I stepped in, even after Alley told me not to. Called Stroud a coward for going after someone who was injured. He didn't like that.

He shoved me, just like he shoved Alley. Before I could even think, I hit him. Punched him right in the face. Alley never warned me that punching bone hurts more than hitting muscle. It worked. Knocked him down.

I guess Alley was right. It really is all in the follow-through.

I think Stroud was too shocked, or maybe too embarrassed, to retaliate. He just left. Didn't even tell Mom.

That's when it happened.

Alley thanked me. Said he appreciated me having his back. High five, and I shocked him.

The second our palms touched, I felt it, like air leaving the room. I saw it happen, the tiny electrode under my skin flexing, the spark leaping from my finger to his.

I didn't mean to do it. The thought just left my head: *He's leaving, and I'm actually going to miss him.* I could see the image of myself in my mind's eye, crying. The sadness bolted, like a fugitive, like it had robbed me.

People fear us. They never ask what it feels like when our own minds betray us. They never consider that maybe we feel just as violated. Our privacy, fragments of our soul, just leave us of their own volition.

Alley flinched, perked up in an instant. My stomach turned. I knew what I did. Worse, I knew what he'd just heard, what he felt. Mom did it to me many times. It's jarring, the overwhelming burst of her reality in my mind.

I waited—for the recoil, the fear, the look that said *you're dangerous.*

Instead, he scoffed. "Weak." Said I could shock him anytime, "if that's all you've got." Then, "You're not getting rid of me that easy."

He took my hand. Not romantic. Not weird. Just steady. Like he wanted me to know he wasn't afraid. He chose me.

We walked back to class, hand in hand.

Acceptance. I don't know what to do with that. I haven't told Mom yet. She'll insist I wear anti-static gloves. I'm not doing it. She might not accept that. At least I know someone will.

Story 02: Dark Space

Most people in Kameon see me as a crackpot, a renegade scientist, not too different from the one who nearly destroyed our world. (That's a story for another day.) Science is often described as a tool to understand the universe. For me, it was always something more. Not a gift or a curiosity. Science is expression, my only pen to write upon the fabric of reality.

I always found the written word too indirect, too easily distorted by the mind reading it. Equations don't twist themselves in transit. Still, science couldn't reach everyone, and silence didn't protect me. So I wrote. I still write, then and now. Not because I trust the reader, but because the absence of the word leaves too much unsaid.

Diary Entry # 08 – Sight Unseen

A.T. 268, Month 15, Day 07 (Tulan Standard Time)

Dad's home. I was excited, and already warning myself not to be.

I should know better. Still, I let myself hope. That was my first mistake.

He arrived mid-morning. Mom lit up. I hovered in the background, trying not to stare like a toddler waiting for a gift. He was ill at ease, more than usual, maybe because this is a work trip home. Talk about an oxymoron.

Alley was already here when Dad came in. I can't say for sure if he made today worse or not. You be the judge, diary. The contrast was stark. Alley moved through the kitchen like it was his. Found the tea, passed out plates, teased Mom about burning the bread again. Dad shuffled around like a guest in his own house. Polite. Tentative. A little too careful with everything he did.

He was warm with me, though. Hugged me like he meant it. Lit up when he saw my models. Gave a few design notes— good ones, actually. Said I had potential. (I don't know if that's a compliment or an insult.)

Then, to my surprise, he invited Alley to join us on the trip to the space station. I didn't want Alley to say yes. I didn't want him to say no, either. At first, he didn't respond. Just watched Dad and me like a puzzle master cracking a master key. He did eventually agree.

Later, we went upstairs so Dad could work. I adjusted the model based on Dad's notes. Simple changes, nothing major. I think Alley was a bit irritated when I went back downstairs to show Dad. I didn't understand why at the time.

Dad was still in the kitchen when I came back. I should say his body was there. He was gone. Buried in reports. Glued to research logs and status updates. I sat next to him with my datapad and tried to keep up. He didn't notice. Side note: the files Alley gave me had better insight than half the army's intel.

I pointed out patterns. Said the dark mist might be reactive to pressure gradients, maybe even manipulated through controlled heat induction or magnetic resonance.

Nothing.

I said it again, louder, clearer. He gave more reaction to a passing wind.

I would have had better luck explaining my thoughts to a pot.

I have no idea how long I was downstairs, but eventually Alley pulled me away. He dried my eyes with the back of his hand. I didn't even notice I had started crying. He walked me to the attic, like a mother explaining cancer to a frightened child. Asked if I was okay. I told him I was. I should have lied. His filter came off.

"He doesn't listen to you," he said. "Not really. You could solve the problem and he'd still pat your head. Ignore you and move on."

I told him to stop. That he didn't know my dad.

Alley didn't back down.

"He's just like your teachers. Smile, nod, ignore." I don't know why that triggered me. Dad was surprisingly similar to Mrs. Fetchvane. Still, he was better than her. He's Dad.

I tried to walk away.

He stopped me. "You think that science station trip is for you? It's not. It's for your mom. To make her feel better."

I wanted to scream. Why wouldn't he drop it? "Then why did he invite you?"

He didn't flinch. "He didn't. I asked your mom."

That stopped me. "What!?" That was his plan all along? Why?

"I asked Aunt Cristal if I could come. She said yes."

"And you're just going to—what? Prove something?" I hated the way my voice broke.

He apologized. Said that based on what I'd told him, he already knew what my dad was. Figured the faster I understood, the better. Said he could prove it.

"You want to know if he sees you? I'll show you. Tell him I shouldn't come. Tell him you don't want me there. Bet you anything he'll still take me. Because it's not about you."

I snapped. Told him this whole "experiment" was cruel and unfair. Told him I hated him.

He shrugged. "Maybe, but it'll work."

Later that night, Dad came to my room. He said sorry. Told me he was distracted. Promised he'd mention my idea to the scientists tomorrow.

I asked if Alley was really coming with us. I tried to keep it subtle. Told him I wanted it to be just us.

He nodded. Didn't even pause. "Of course he's coming." That was it. No hesitation. No check-in with me.

He loves me. I know that, but he doesn't value what I bring to the table.

Alley said as much before he left. "I'm not saying he doesn't love you, Maria. I think he really does." I remember the way he looked into my eyes, probably the most sincere I have ever seen him. I honestly didn't think he was capable of being sincere in that way about anything but a fight before this.

"He just doesn't respect your mind."

That hurt more than anything else. The truth. I'm not sure I'll ever unhear it. "You're just his daughter."

Vault Diary - Hypothesis Oblivion

Diary Entry # 09 – Nobody's Daughter

A.T. 268, Month 15, Day 09 (Tulan Standard Time)

I was excited for today, until I woke up. The image of Alley hovering haunted my morning routine. Why did he have to be right? I know he would never taunt me, but I could still feel his condescending glare following me. A hint of what was to come.

Alley showed up early, of course. He looked excited, like he genuinely wanted to be part of today. I ignored him until we had to go.

I said, maybe shouted, that I didn't want him coming. Mom was shocked. Reprimanded me. So did Dad. The trip was delayed twenty minutes for a full-blown morality committee. Both parents went in on how selfish I was.

Alley was the only one who defended me. Never mentioned his experiment, but stood up for me. The boy I rejected. Said it was okay. Said he could walk home. His home is twenty miles away.

I cracked. Not for Mom. Not for Dad. For him. Because somehow, he understands me. He didn't make a scene. Didn't guilt me. Didn't take it personally. He just accepted it and still stood beside me.

I'm in my house, surrounded by family, and the only one actually here for me is someone I met less than two months ago. Let that sink in. This is apparently my life now.

Objective truth, I hate you.

The trip to the station was fine. Uneventful. Smooth docking. Minimal turbulence. Still a miracle to me, crossing planets like it's nothing.

I can't imagine living before space travel, stuck on your birth planet forever. Fine if you're from Alphaeus or Kameon C. But if you drew Tula or Magosia? You'd be trapped in a wasteland of prairies. No way out.

The scientists were focused on the gas cloud. Their scanners worked on the outskirts but degraded the deeper they pushed.

They walked me through their system. Standard tech. Nothing revolutionary. I could build a weaker version myself. I still can't understand how they didn't see the issue.

The problem wasn't the scanner, it was the gas. They were trying to see through it instead of moving it. I came up with three ways to part the gas using common local materials.

When I went to tell Dad, he was in a meeting with the Executive General Board, the one group in the army that outranked him, save the Commander himself. Most of them were there by video conference, but Executive General Towelain was there in person. I'd met him before. He used to be the Executive General in charge of Scientific Research before Perrian took over. Now he handles diplomacy and special operations.

He always had a thing for Mom, never subtle about it. I never understood why Dad didn't seem to care. He even invited Towelain over once. Said it was funny watching him try to win Mom over. Annoying, but possibly useful.

When Dad was leaving his meeting, I made sure to slip in right after the video call disconnected so I could tell him my ideas in front of General Towelain. Maybe he would push for it if Dad kept ignoring me. It seemed to work at first, but not in the way I intended.

Dad tried to wave me off before I could make my suggestion, but Towelain shushed him and pulled rank. He knelt down to ask how I would deal with the issue. It was so condescending. That was the last thing I wanted. I knew I would never hear the end of it. Dad was going to kill me, but I had to explain now. Towelain outranked my father, so technically, I was under orders. Dad listened and even seemed a bit impressed when I explained how the process might work.

All Towelain said was, "Talented kid you've got there. Just like her mother." Then he gave me a wink before leaving without another word. Cringe. Remind me never to try to strong-arm my dad again.

Either way, Dad said he'd bring it up to the science team. I was waiting for him to skin me alive for embarrassing him in front of his superior officer, but he never said a word.

He never said a word to the science team either.

When we met the science corps, he introduced me and Alley, took their report, and asked some questions. That was it. I tried to add my thoughts, but he shut me down quickly.

He told them to disregard me, like I wasn't even in the room. At the time, I felt I deserved that, so I let it go.

Alley didn't. He called Dad out in front of everyone. He didn't raise his voice, just asked why I was brought at all if I wasn't allowed to speak. He asked if Dad knew how hard I'd worked to help him, told him to ask me anything about dark space.

Dad didn't even try. He just had Alley escorted to our waiting transport, straight back to the ship to wait all day.

Then Dad turned to me and said, "You were right not to want him here."

I couldn't believe him.

He humiliated the only person who stood up for me, then acted like that proved a point. I did humiliate him, but...

We haven't spoken since. Dad's still in the house, still walking the halls, still pretending nothing's wrong. He hasn't asked why I won't talk to him. He may not even notice. He probably wouldn't understand even if I told him.

I know he cares.
I think he does.
I hope he does.

Love isn't the same thing as respect. Is Alley the only one who sees the difference? I owe him an apology. He might be the only person in my life who really sees me.

I should stop crying. I'm smudging the ink.

I'll write more tomorrow, diary.
Promise.

Diary Entry # 10 – Hypothesis: Ignored

A.T. 268, Month 15, Day 12 (Tulan Standard Time)

I apologized to Alley. He didn't care. Said that's what power does to adults. That his whole goal was to be immune to it, to reach a place where people couldn't hurt him. Not because he was invincible, but because he didn't play the game.

"If that means I grow up with no power at all, then so be it." He wasn't offended, just tired.

Dad spent the entire day yesterday buried in reports again. I spent the entire day trying to change his mind, trying to get him to give my idea a chance. Nothing.

Alley told me to give it up. "His loss," he said. He's right, I know. But if I give up now, I'll always be ignored.

I thought about it all night. This morning, I made a decision.

I'm going to prove it.

I know how to replicate the black gas in the void. It's not even that complex. The right chemical balance, the right containment, the right apparatus, and I can simulate it here. If I can create it and control it, then my method works. That's it. That's proof.

He can't ignore proof.

Alley called me insane, then offered to help.

We spent all day acquiring the right chemicals. I triple-checked every reaction and every potential instability. Spent my nights studying formulas, my days building and modifying the containment arm.

It was ready tonight, but Alley was supposed to go home.

Alley wanted to wait until morning. I said no. He sighed and left.

I started the experiment. The apparatus worked. The gas formed, heavy and dark in the chamber. I linked the coil, magnetized the control arm, and...

It moved.

The gas moved. I manipulated it, like a puppet on a string. Even when I pushed it out of the primary vessel, it stayed tethered to my control arm. Obedient. Responsive.

It was working. I was right.

I was just about to release the gas and shut it down when something went wrong. There was a sound, like a snap and a burst of air, then pressure.

It was like I'd been punched in the chest by the sky itself. I remember the window sill slamming into my spine, then the floor, then nothing. I remember my last thought before I blacked out, a silent prayer that one shard of glass had hit my back. If I didn't break the window, that meant I was lying on the floor of a sealed lab filled with toxic gas.

Nothing.

I blacked out fully expecting never to wake up.

I shouldn't be alive.

Alley pulled me out of there. He came back to check on me. I can only imagine how freaked out he must have been, walking into a room full of black gas. Uncontained. Unstable. Toxic. He knew what was in there. I can't believe he did it. I'm ashamed to say I don't know if I would have.

There's a hazmat team at the house now. I'm in the hospital.

The doctors say I'll be fine. They won't answer my questions.

No one is telling me how Alley is. They keep dodging, changing the subject. Mom won't meet my eyes. Dad won't talk to me. He's holding me, drying my tears on his uniform. He always said that was what his shoulder was for, uniform or no.

I'm terrified.

I gave everything I had. No one would even consider my idea without proof.

And I proved it.

Now it doesn't matter. I just need to know that Alley's okay.

Why won't anyone just tell me?

He can't be... because of me.

Diary Entry # 11 – Collateral

A.T. 268, Month 15, Day 13 (Tulan Standard Time)

They brought Alley into my room this morning. He's out of intensive care.

His breathing was ragged. He barely spoke. I'm just glad he's alive. If he'd died, I'd have to follow just to kill him again for being so stupid. The gas ravaged his lungs. I'd be in the same state if the blast hadn't knocked me to the floor before the chamber ruptured. I still can't believe he pulled me out. I owe him my life. I'm still processing that. He'll have a joke for it when he recovers.

Aunt Linda came not long after. She didn't look at me right away, just checked on Alley — his monitors, his temperature, his breathing.

When I tried to speak, Mom started to shush me.

Aunt Linda stopped her. "Let her apologize." She didn't sound angry.

I said I was sorry. She nodded. "It's not your fault, Maria. You're a child, trying to help. I know how much work you both put into that project. Alley paid two months' allowance for all the information he got for you." She had the faintest smile, like the memory gave her a second of peace. I wish she could have stayed there. Instead, she turned on my parents.

"It's you two. You didn't listen to her. Now my boy is in this bed because of it." She put every drop of vitriol she could conjure into that statement. It wasn't much, but she had nothing left.

She sat beside Alley and didn't say another word.

It took me a second to realize what had just happened. Aunt Linda defended me. Maybe not gently, certainly not the way I wanted — but she did. Under any other circumstance, it would have made me feel validated. Here, it struck like a dagger to the chest. It's not my parents' fault he's barely breathing. It's mine. I messed up somehow. I turned our attic into a biohazard.

Why didn't he just leave me there?

Alley woke up this afternoon. Eyes half-open. Could barely move. I've never seen him so weak.

"Did the experiment work? What happened?"

I told him it didn't. That it was a failure. Thirty seconds of control means nothing if the system explodes after that. He asked what went wrong. I couldn't answer. I just stared at him, trying not to cry again.

He coughed, tried to laugh. Worst decision of the day. I thought he'd vomit out a lung.

"I already took the hit for this smoke controller. You better figure it out."

That was all he said. I don't think he meant it as an order.

Doesn't matter.

He asked.

I'll deliver.

No excuses.

They discharged me that evening. The hazmat team finished clearing the attic. The room's still intact. The explosion did what it was supposed to, released pressure into the controller. The fault wasn't the gas.

It was the seal. The system failed because I didn't bleed the pressure. At least, I think that's it.

I tried to tell Mom and Dad. Tried to explain the fix, how to reinforce the containment junctions, how to stagger the pressure release. They told me to drop it. Said it was too dangerous. That I needed rest. That it was over.

Later that night, they came into my room. Apologized. No, Mom apologized. Dad just stood there, still silent. She said they were scared, that they should have listened sooner. Told me I could explain it all later, then insisted I let it go.

Let it go!? After everything?

What do I have to do!? They're still not listening.

Diary Entry # 12 – Demonstration

A.T. 268, Month 15, Day 14 (Tulan Standard Time)

I decided to run a second experiment.

Mom is going to kill me. Slowly. If the gas doesn't get me first. There's no version of this where she doesn't find out. The release valve alone makes enough noise to wake the dead. Even with soundproofing and the nozzle angled out the window, it won't be quiet.

I'll do it anyway.

I gathered the materials again. Built in a failsafe this time in case of rupture. Spent the whole day tweaking the pressure regulator and triple-checking the sequence. Thank God Mom had to work with the farmhands all day. I spent half the day terrified she would come to the lab while I was rebuilding the apparatus. She came once, but I had just enough time to throw a sheet over it. I can't believe that worked.

Dinner just finished and Mom's tucked me in. It took almost ten minutes to wriggle out of the covers. She's worried about me. She's probably right. I'll have to wait until after midnight to start, otherwise she'll shut me down.

Wish me luck, diary.

Vault Diary - Hypothesis Oblivion

Diary Update:

Everything went according to plan. I started the machine. My hands were shaking, not from fear of the gas, but from fear of being right and still being ignored.

The apparatus generated the gas like before. I activated the control arm, and it was everything I imagined.

The gas formed, dense, dark, compliant. The control arm was even more precise than my last iteration. I twisted the dark mist into a coil. A spiral. A pentagon. I was having fun. .. until.

The release valve shrieked. Loud, piercing, grating. I knew it would happen eventually. I thought I would have more time. One minute later, Mom was pounding on the attic door.

She knocked it open a moment later, actually ripped it off the hinge. (I don't see a replacement coming any time soon.) I have never been more terrified in my life. I would take the toxic gas and a den of wolves over the woman I saw raging in that doorway. I barely got a word in. She yelled on entry. Her first order was drowned out by the sound of the broken door.

I kept moving the gas, controlling the pressure, shaping the flow. She didn't notice until I started writing with it. I drew one phrase:

"Mom. Look."

She froze. Mid-sentence. Mid-scolding.

I stood there, holding galactic poison in my hand, spelling her name with it like it was ink. Then, for the first time, I felt safe.

I wrote, "Thank you." I opened the window and let it go. The gas drifted into the sky, dissolving harmlessly into the upper atmosphere.

She didn't move. I think she couldn't speak. When she finally did,

"How did you do that?"

There was awe in her voice. Real awe. It only lasted a second.

"Go to your room."

The order came subdued. I made the mistake of staying a second too long.

"GO!"

So that's it. No review. No mention of it to Dad. Just punishment. I took off the control arm and walked out, slow. I had something to say. I knew I only had from the wall to the door to say it.

I told her I knew what I did was wrong. That I was ready to accept the consequences. I only asked for one thing:

"Please send the data to the science station."

She didn't respond.

Vault Diary - Hypothesis Oblivion

This morning, I tried talking to Dad. Yes, now he can talk. He didn't even ask how I was. Said I'd broken the agreement. Didn't ask how the experiment went. Just said rules are rules, safety comes first.

I'm still stuck on how I broke the agreement. I never recall agreeing to anything. Agreements require discussions, and we never had one of those.

What does it take for them to see me? Hear me? Does it matter that I was doing this for him? I'm still invisible.

Now what?

I have data, but no one will review it.
I have results, but no one will analyze it.
I have reports, but no one will read it.

I'm not allowed in the lab. Not allowed to work. Not allowed to speak.

And I'm not sorry. Not anymore.

Diary Entry # 13 – Recognition

A.T. 268, Month 15, Day 20 (Tulan Standard Time)

Alley came over today. It must have been hard for him. He's still recovering. I know Mom only let it happen to prove he was alive. She let it slip that his condition got worse after I was discharged. I hadn't seen him in days. I was starting to imagine the worst.

"I told the doctors not to release my good luck charm," he said. His laugh is still weak. Best sound I've heard in so long. It still hurts him to breathe.

I told him everything: about the second experiment, that I proved it, that my method works. That no one would send the data. I told him he was right. No one listens. It doesn't matter.

I thought he'd tell me to try again, push me to find another way. He didn't. He just said, "You did good, kid." I would have made him pay for that "kid" jab, but he's too weak to defend himself right now. He had to leave right after. Honestly, I felt bad that he came, even if it meant the world to see him. It looked like the effort took everything he had.

Aunt Linda saw me before she took him home. I apologized again. She didn't let me finish.

"It's not your fault," she said. "But be more careful next time." It was as stern as she ever was with me. They both told me to rest, like I had a choice. I'm grounded.

A few hours later, Dad came upstairs. Told me we'd talk about punishment later. I was insubordinate. The trip he planned to Liviton Space Port was cancelled. Who cares? Why would I want to go anywhere with him, just to be ignored?

I stayed in bed for half the day. I've been numb ever since I was grounded, and seeing Alley didn't make me feel any better. Mom lifted the ban on my lab, so I went up to the attic to clean it.

(Okay, fine. I'm starting to like a clean lab.)

Problem: it was already clean. Too clean. My research was gone. All my work. No notes. No schematics. No data.

I don't know what came over me. A rage filled me before my brain could even process it. I ran downstairs and found Mom in the kitchen. I started yelling at her. What did you do to my lab? How could you destroy all my research? That apparatus took ages to construct! Do you realize what you've done?

I realized one second too late just how badly I had messed up. When I started yelling, she was too confused to react. When I ran out of steam, she filled up with lava. She didn't say a word at first, just grabbed my shirt. Two near-death experiences in as many weeks.

After making sure I knew my place at the bottom of the food chain in the House of Maze, she answered my questions. She had my lab cleaned out. Gave specific instructions that my papers were not to be touched. She'd hired a team to remove the apparatus to the storage shed.

I checked as soon as she said it. Left her mid-sentence. It wasn't there. Neither model. When I told her, she said nothing.

I lost it again. Yelled. Loud. Told her she destroyed everything. That maybe if they actually listened, really listened, none of this would have happened. She swore she didn't touch my notes and made sure my machines were preserved.

She wasn't lying. I know her face when she tries to lie. That impossible twitch in her eyes, like her brain short-circuits mid-sentence. It wasn't there. Just exhaustion. Besides, "no lying" is the one rule I can nail her for just as easily as she can get me.

She told me to watch my tone. I did cross a line, but I was already grounded. Alley wasn't coming back until he recovered. What else could she really do? (What is wrong with me? She could do plenty. The last thing I ever want to do is test her creativity in that realm.) She sent me to my room.

"When I catch the thief, you might want to thank him. He's the only reason you're alive." She promised to find my machines.

Later that evening, Dad came home. He wasn't alone.

He brought two men in uniforms, General Towelain and a man in a lab coat. I ignored them at first. I was on my way to my room when Dad stopped me.

Vault Diary - Hypothesis Oblivion

"You remember Executive General Towelain," Dad reintroduced us. I wasn't sure I wanted to. The last time I saw him, I humiliated my father, who was more than happy to return the favor. That said, the Executive General didn't look like he wanted to be there either.

I tried to put on what Mom expects from me when we have such important company: formal bows and courtesy. He made it clear he had no interest in speaking to me. When I bowed, he looked away, like the sight of me made his stomach turn. He didn't speak, just scoffed loud enough to make my father flinch. Dad looked ready to hit him.

Who killed his dog?

It was the reaction I'd expect from a child forced to make up with a bully after a fight. It wasn't scary, just... actually made me appreciate my mother teaching me basic respect.

Dad's other guest more than made up for it.

"This is Dr. Vandire Childs," Dad said, trying his best to recover from General Snob. "Scientific lead of the Dark Souls Project."

I froze. That's a code name. Civilians don't hear code names.

Dr. Childs smiled and offered his hand. Said it was an honor to meet me. Told me he'd read my work — my work — and was blown away.

He pulled out a paper, ready for publication. My name was on top.

Lead Scientist.

Below it: my research. Cleaned up, formatted, annotated, but still mine. Every data point. Every diagram. Right there. Beside it were the station's replication results. Full confirmation.

"You're meticulous," he said. "Who taught you to document like this?" I pointed him to the books I studied, the ones no one ever thought I'd finished.

I ran to Dad. Hugged him. Thanked him for sending the work.

He pulled back. More like pushed me away. Not harsh, not cold, just broken. Like the weight of my gratitude hurt more than my disappointment ever could. He looked defeated. Wouldn't meet my eyes.

"I didn't." That's all he said. The rest of the night, he barely spoke. He escorted General Towelain out after dinner.

Mom tried to send me to bed after dinner, but Dad overruled her. Said I could stay up and talk to Dr. Childs as long as needed. So we did. For hours.

Dr. Childs asked questions. Took notes. Treated me like a colleague. Not a prodigy. Not a child. Not a daughter. An equal.

It was three in the morning when Mom finally stepped in.

"She may be a genius, but she's still a child. Her mother is cutting you off. Take your complaint to the Lieutenant General if you wish. I outrank him."

Dr. Childs bowed to both of us. "Then I'll be back in the morning." He's not returning to the station. He wants to stay, to go over more work with me.

"I'll make more progress down here than up there."

Tonight, I feel something.

Not joy.
Not exactly.
But close.

Diary Entry # 14 – Too Little, Too Late

A.T. 268, Month 15, Day 21 (Tulan Standard Time)

Most daughters live for the day their fathers say they're proud of them.

Dads of the world—if you ever read this:

TELL YOUR KIDS YOU'RE PROUD OF THEM.

Seriously. We don't hear it enough. Most of us don't hear it at all.

That said, it's strange. My dad said he was proud of me today. It didn't make me feel any better. Maybe because it's so easy for him to say now, when it costs him nothing.

If he'd said it in the beginning, when I was desperate for it, maybe I would've melted. Maybe I would've cried. Maybe it would've meant the world. Now it just feels like he's trying to dig himself out of a hole.

He sees me now. Sure. But only because I locked him in a room full of pictures of me screaming *"NOTICE ME."* It shouldn't take all that. Why did I have to compete with the military's top minds just to get my father to realize I exist?

Now that I have his attention, I don't even want it.

I perked up when Dr. Childs arrived today. He didn't come empty-handed. He brought half a lab with him: a full chemistry set, containment tools, shielding rigs, and a transparent chemical refrigerator that glows blue.

He caught me staring. "Sorry about the blue glow," he said. He doesn't understand. That case is mine now. Forever.

Then he pulled something smooth and aqua-blue from a garment bag. Sleek. A lab coat. He unfolded it and placed it on my shoulders like he was dressing royalty. Said it matched the color of my brilliance.

It was the first time I wore something that felt like *me*, not a version of me my parents wanted. Just me.

We spent half the day setting up. He was just like Alley; everything had to be organized. But he let me lead. Guided, never overstepped. Said I reminded him of his daughter, Sarah.

We went over the project, documented findings, and compared data. He had no issue showing where their results diverged from mine—only curiosity. Clarity. We built parameters for two new experiments. The science team added multiple outlet valves to my old design. Their design reduced pressure on the controller by 60%, dramatically lowering the chance of a critical overload. Apparently, what happened to me is a very common mistake: underestimating pressure buildup.

I wonder how common Alley is. Has to be one in a million. Probably rarer.

Childs gave me a new book. A lab manual with hundreds of pages on safety thresholds and proper procedures. The kind of book that could've kept me out of the hospital.

Then he invited me to speak with the team. Not observe. Not shadow. Speak.

I almost laughed. I declined. "I'm still grounded."

He looked disappointed but nodded. "You're still a kid."

"I wish I could be more help."

He grinned. "No, you're speaking. You're the lead scientist on this part of the project. I literally can't take no for an answer. Even your mom couldn't override that."

I asked him not to push. The last thing I wanted was for Towelain to pull rank on my parents again. He said my dad actually wanted me to present. Got Mom to approve. Brought it to the Commander of the Kameonic Army after Towelain objected. He was the one who pushed it through.

When he left, I just sat there, wondering. Why did I do all this? Dad gets two extra days off now that the team has what they need. I'm grounded. What can I do with that? He did fight for me. He is proud of me. Who cares? Maybe I did once. Not anymore. His "I'm proud of you" haunts me more than anything. Why?

It took me until after I was sent to bed to figure it out. I heard Mom and Dad talking downstairs. Mom was actually defending me for once. Said I was desperate for his approval. (Uh, no. I'd settle for him acknowledging my existence in my presence.) She said the whole thing happened because he didn't give me the attention I needed. Amazing how she managed to ignore her role in that, but I digress.

Then he said it. The one thing I wish I could unhear: "I just can't believe my eleven-year-old daughter could figure this out.

I mean… she's eleven."

He didn't say it to be cruel. It still stung. To Dr. Childs, I'm a colleague. My age is a footnote, an insignificant variable. To my parents, it's a barrier. A reason not to listen.

I get it. I really do. On the other hand, I'm tired of waiting for time to validate me. I'm not asking them to pretend I'm an adult. I just wish they could see what Dr. Childs sees.

A person.
With thoughts. With ideas. With opinions.

Alley sees it. Why can't they?

He's known me for one month, and sometimes I think he gets me more than my own blood.

Story 003: The Tournament

Most parents love their kids. Self-preservation. Kids love their parents for the same reason. The first love that's earned is friendship. I learned early that friendship was overrated. Family is fleeting. The only person I could rely on to love me was me.

Alley changed my life in more ways than I like to admit. He was closer than a friend, closer than a brother. Love has a price in all dimensions. Most of the time, the cost is too high for the merchandise.

Vault Diary - Hypothesis Oblivion

Diary Entry # 15 – Preparing for the Tournament

A.T. 269, Month 1, Day 14 (Tulan Standard Time)

Expect to hear a lot about Alley this month.

I've been neck-deep in my energy research and just started dabbling in robotics. Alley's been... obsessed. He's training for the Mast Tournament like his life depends on it. I've never seen anyone work so hard. It's inspiring and scary at the same time.

He's up before Rostain, running five miles into the sunrise. Most days, he shows up just before breakfast.

He's been staying here a few weeks; our terrain's better for training, and mornings start with Aunt Linda in the kitchen. Chef-level breakfast. Honestly, I think it's the only reason no one's complained.

Sorry, Mom. Aunt Linda's the superior cook, hands down. (Not that Mom ever competed.)

In the evening, Alley trains me. Basic combat. How to punch. How to kick. How not to fall flat on my face when I block. I'm shocked he wants me to spar at all, but he says teaching me helps him lock in his fundamentals. He says it forces him to slow down and analyze everything again.

(Translation: I'm a terrible opponent, but at least I'm educational.)

Still haven't landed a punch. I've learned a lot about balance and reaction timing. Kinesiology, right? Whatever. He's given everything to the goal. He's falling behind in every class, even writing. Aunt Linda has mandated I study with him an hour a day, and he won't let it go one minute past the hour no matter how bad he needs it.

He's nearing his peak.

Lorenz-I is unable to train him anymore. He's off on a trip and won't be back until a few days before the tournament. Alley needs a new serious sparring partner.

I think I have a solution.

There's this Chan roboticist, Corten Zenith. Bit of a legend. I found fragments of his archived research buried in an old database. Might've bypassed some security protocols, but no one will ever know. They weren't even that secure.

He had a theoretical model for something called a Zolphoid, an autonomous drone. There's nothing in the design that says "sparring bot," but I'm pretty sure I can make it into one. If I integrate basic AI and adaptive feedback, it could match Alley's speed and learn from each bout.

I told Alley about it. Now he's too excited. He doesn't seem to care how dangerous it is or how close I am to turning it on him. If he leans over my shoulder one more time, I swear I'll have his precious drones send him to the trauma center.

I'm trying to be patient, diary, but he is trying me. I know this is important to him, but he doesn't know what he's asking. Portable technology of this complexity is rare and hard to construct; I can't connect it to the house, school, or barn's main power drive, so I had to custom build, charge, and maintain each of the batteries myself. The control chips and power storage modules are expensive. I can cover them with my contest winnings. That might cover all of it, but I don't really need the money anyway. The biggest problem is, drones don't understand "too fast" or "too hard." To them, 2 mph and 200 mph are just energy differentials.

I had to stop him from field testing my first drone. That kick would have taken his head off, blocked or not. (I'd appreciate the quiet, for two seconds, before the devastation hit.) I feel like maybe I should call this off, but Alley would never forgive me.

I think I've got the equations right this time. I've finally synthesized an alloy with the right durability. I've got the safety gear. I'll triple-check everything.

If I do this right, Alley will have the sparring partner he needs. It'll be great. I just hope I can finish in time for the tournament.

I'm giving it a week. Let's be honest, it'll take two. If I mess this up, he won't get another chance.

Diary Entry # 16 - Machines That Learn

A.T. 269, Month 1, Day 30 (Tulan Standard Time)

I was partially right. It took a week and a half to build the Zolphoid drone. Once everything was calibrated, making more was easy. I finished six. With twenty-two days left until the tournament, I'm betting that by the time Lorenz-I is back, he won't stand a chance.

The Mast Tournament is split into two phases. Day One is one-on-one, double elimination. Day Two is a full-scale, six-fighter battle royale. If Alley's going to survive, he needs to train for both. Right now, he's struggling with just one.

That's not a dig at him; it's a credit to the AI. I actually had to toggle their learning curves down. They were improving faster than any fighter could realistically adapt. I made them slower, less reactive, more predictable.

Alley was annoyed. "If I can't beat the bot at its best, what's the point of training?"

How about avoiding a shattered rib cage? Is that reason enough? He still doesn't understand; this thing could kill him. He's not invincible, though he can take a hit better than I calculated was possible given his metrics. I found that out the hard way on day two of live testing, when the safeguards failed. Try explaining those bruises to Aunt Linda. She thought I was helping by attacking him with a bat. (Not that far from the truth.)

They're still faster than any person. Way faster.

He's been training with them every day. Once during school, he snuck into their storage shed during lunch and ran a simulation without me. That irritated me. I went off on him. I can't believe how much of my mom I channeled in that moment. That was the second time I almost shut this whole thing down. One more time and I pull the plug. I already told him he's not allowed to die because of me.

He promised. But we both know promises are cheap right now.

Something about him is starting to worry me. More than before. He's been obsessed with this tournament ever since the start of the year. That part I've gotten used to. I keep thinking once this tournament is over, I'll get my friend back. I'm not so sure anymore.

Right now, I am scared he'll kill himself somehow before he even steps onto the tournament floor. Or someone else. He's getting more aggressive lately. It's leaking into everything. He almost got into a fight with Stroud over nothing. Same old Stroud: snide comments, subtle digs. Stroud hates Aquians. A lot of people do. But Alley's always been good at ignoring him.

This time? He wasn't ignoring anything. He looked like he wanted to do more than respond. The only reason he didn't hit him was because I stepped in front of Stroud. He almost hit me instead. Ran off when he realized what he'd done. Didn't talk to me till the next day, and didn't address what happened at all. What is wrong with him?

On a side note, I put myself in harm's way for Stroud. I will make Alley suffer for that one when this tournament is done.

Mom pulled me aside today and thanked me for helping Alley. Said it meant a lot to Uncle Quince. Apparently he once qualified for the Mast Tournament. Is that why Alley is so obsessed?

Uncle Quince said the tournament's brutal. Anything goes. Told me I didn't have to go.

Of course I'll go. Alley came to my model presentation. I know that was torture.

I have a funny feeling, but I can't pinpoint why. Strange thing happened today: a farmhand caught sight of us moving the drones. Alley got weird. Started stuttering. He couldn't focus for the rest of the session. Got angry with me when I tried to correct him. He's never been self-conscious like that.

Something's not right.

I'm starting to wonder if I'll have to sabotage this tournament just to save what's left of him.

Vault Diary - Hypothesis Oblivion

Diary Entry # 17 – He Knew

A.T. 269, Month 1, Day 31 (Tulan Standard Time)

I'm dead. Capital-D dead.

If by some miracle I survive whatever comes next, I'm going to find Alley and kill him. I may get a death sentence for that, but at least I'll die with a smile on my face.

He knew exactly what he was doing, what he tricked me into doing. He let me do it anyway.

This morning, I woke up to both of my parents standing in my room, staring at me like someone died. Not exactly a warm wake-up call. Mom sat on the edge of my bed, tense and quiet. Dad stood over me, arms crossed, jaw locked, eyes cold. Breathing hard. Glaring.

For a second, I thought they'd fought with each other. When Dad said my name, I knew whose funeral I was attending. Mine.

He held something up between his fingers: a control chip, the kind you only see inside machines. In his other hand was the partially crushed head of one of my combat drones. It still had the blue line across the right eye, my alignment marker. From the look of it, he blasted its face off with a shield arm cannon. He must have activated it on his own somehow. Judging by the impact marks, my drone got a few hits in before he blew its face off.

How did he activate it? I know I locked up all the drones and shut them down last night after Alley left. He came back? He promised he wouldn't.

"Did you build this?" he asked.

I stared at it. At the chip. At the drone's head, or what was left of it. Did I build a device that could have killed my father? What was my dad going to do to me?

For one awful second, I didn't answer. Not because I didn't know. Something in me did know, and worse, this wasn't just about me. This was about Alley.

Thirty seconds passed. Dad grabbed my pajamas and pulled me close, his death stare penetrating my soul.

"Maria!?"

I don't know what kept me silent, but I wish I'd just confessed. My mother tapped the back of my neck. Nalaxon extended. A moment later, she was in, hacking my mind like a computer. She rifled through my thoughts: days in the attic, our conversations, my diary. Every private thought I'd tucked away recoiled, then spilled out through my eyes, ripped free by her will. My autonomy was gone in a flash.

When I felt the cold spike retract, I confessed. I'd rather say it myself.

"Yes. I built it."

Dad didn't react. He just told me to get dressed and meet him downstairs. I think he was honestly surprised. Mom tried to apologize.

"Don't talk to me." That's all I could say. I don't care what trouble I'm in; she and I are done. Stealing thoughts like that is strictly forbidden among Aquians, the worst kind of violation.

"Maria, mind your tone." Really? She had the audacity to respond!?

"Mib. Don't. Talk to me." I stormed out before she could say anything else. I locked myself in the bathroom for half an hour. Between my own fury and the firing squad charging their arm cannons downstairs to finish me off, I needed time to write my will. If my mother didn't kill me for how I spoke to her, my father would because my drones tried to kill him.

When I got to the kitchen, Mom and Dad were dressed. Dad in his military uniform. Mom in her Inquisitor's robes. I hadn't seen them in ages. A book waited on the table, thick, with a military seal on the front. Page 752 was already open, a red marker tucked to the side. Mom hovered in the kitchen, glaring in the background.

Dad didn't say anything. Just pointed.

"Chan-Army Peace Treaty, Clause 72, Subsection 210b: Neither the Army nor Chan, nor either of their citizens, shall construct autonomous drones for use in combat, construction, or any functional capacity without prior approval from a joint delegation of the Chan and Kameonic Army, subject to override only by the Chan Master or the Army Commander."

Then the front door opened. Footsteps. Alley. Fresh from his morning run, sweat still on his forehead. He stepped into the room and froze.

"…Sir?"

That one word said everything. Dad didn't even look at him. He just said, low and even, "Get out."

Alley looked at me, then the table, then the chip. The drone's head was still in Dad's hand. His mouth opened, then closed, like he didn't know which truth to start with.

"I—I didn't—"

I tried to ask Alley if he'd snuck into the storage shed to fight the drone, but Dad shut me up as soon as he heard the word "training." Mom activated from the depths of the kitchen, and I think the pan she was holding was meant for Alley's face.

"You had my daughter build you a battle drone for training?" I had never heard that voice from Mom before. Dad shut everything down.

"Get out!" This time, Alley did. Fast. No goodbye.

I stared at the page, the words, the chip. It felt radioactive.

Dad sighed, his glare dissolving into something I couldn't place.

"Go to school. Go home. Go to bed.
No lab. No training. No life."

Vault Diary - Hypothesis Oblivion

That was it. No lecture. No yelling. Just a total shutdown. Alley didn't show up at school. Aunt Linda hasn't heard from him either. I heard Mom talking with her. She's worried sick, and honestly, I don't care. I hope a wolf tears him to shreds.

He knew those drones were illegal. I see it now. I saw it in his eyes when Dad walked in. He was terrified before he even saw the drone's severed head. He knew this could come. He never told me. He used me. He let me build the drones, watched me agonize over every line, every error. Worrying that if I made a mistake, it would hurt HIM. Knowing full well I was breaking interplanetary law. Did he think I'd cover for him? He didn't need to ask. I already did.

I still can't believe Mom stole my thoughts. I can't believe I called her a Mib.

Why did he do this to me?
Because of that stupid tournament?
Because he wanted to win that badly?

I need to talk to him. I need to know. Because if this was all about winning, then I *will* crank those last five drones to full power, bypass every safeguard I put in them, and send every last one of them to kill him. Let's see if his training paid off. I hope it was worth it. I should have known better than to trust him.

Stroud was worse than usual today. Actually, no, he wasn't. Slurs, bullying, the usual. If this is what friendship looks like, I'll take Stroud. At least he doesn't pretend to be anything else.

Let him call me a Mib. He's not wrong. I wish I was. If I could invade minds, Alley's would be first. So I could tear it apart, piece by piece.

Vault Diary - Hypothesis Oblivion

Diary Entry # 18 – Pieces I Can't Destroy

A.T. 269, Month 1, Day 32 (Tulan Standard Time)

Dad ordered me to destroy the drones. He said he talked it over with the Chan and the Army. If it had been anyone else, we'd probably all be in a cell by now. I almost prefer that. At least Alley would get what he deserves.

I had to disclose how I got my hands on Corten Zenith's design theories and base shell specifications. I was a little dodgy about hacking the archive backlog files. Dad didn't push. I think he knew he didn't want to hear it officially.

Dad banned me from the lab for a month. No models. No experiments. He sealed the lab door himself. Mom and Dad haven't talked to me since. Honestly, I haven't talked to either of them. I don't know if I want to.

What Alley did was unforgivable, but Mom? That was somehow worse. Mom has transmitted thoughts before, never stolen. Always swore she never would. She didn't just break her word; she didn't hesitate. I can't trust her. I can't trust Alley. I can't trust Dad. I guess I can't trust anyone. Worse, my dad is actually the most reasonable of them all.

I have to admit, this is more alone than even I want to be. The only person who talks to me now is the person who insults me every day.

I never thought I'd appreciate Stroud. I had a conversation with him today. A real conversation. For the first time ever, I actually hate my life.

Alley still hasn't come back to school. I've seen him, though—lurking behind the trees near the storage closet behind the school tower. Always watching. The second I spot him, he bolts. Never seen him so deflated. I'm glad.

Apparently, he's still attending anatomy—the one class we don't share.

Today, I took a long bathroom break near the end of last period. Found his classroom. Walked right in like I owned the place.

"Mistress Maze needs to see Alejandro in her office," I said.

The teacher blinked, nodded, and didn't even question it.

Alley knew I was bluffing. He played along. He always plays along.

We didn't go to Mom's office. We just walked.

He didn't deny it. Didn't even try. I asked him why.

His answer? There was no good reason. Nothing to justify it. He did it for his father. He said it was the one summit Uncle Quince could never climb: the title of the Mast Master. After his injury, Uncle Quince knew he would never fight at full strength again, so Alley promised to win the tournament for him. I never could tell Uncle Quince even had an injury, but Dad mentioned it from time to time.

Alley walked me back to class. Told me to leave him alone, not to get in more trouble because of him.

He said he didn't deserve a friend like me.

He could switch classes, drop out of the tournament.

He said he was sorry he ruined my life.

I could tell he meant it. That he hated what this cost me. It didn't make it better. Honestly, he should feel sorry. I was furious. Still am. That said, I didn't want that apology. I didn't ask for it, and it didn't fix anything.

A third-grade group came up a minute later, and we had to run to the library to avoid getting caught. There was a moment, running away from those overgrown toddlers, that almost felt like us before this whole thing. I half wish we were still running. I wish I could forget.

When we were finally alone again, we stood staring at each other. I don't think we knew what to say. There is no protocol for resolving betrayal. What snapped me out of it? He asked me to "say something."

I slapped him. It was all I could do. Start his torture. He can't escape me that easily. I snatched his shirt and pulled him close. What came over me, I will never know.

"You don't get to transfer."

"You don't get to skip school. I need you in that class so I can actively torture and hate you. Got that?!"

I pushed him away and left. He just stood there, dumbfounded. Fine by me, but I didn't know if he still planned to disappear.

So I let him know it was off the table:
"And you don't get to drop out of the tournament."

Alley insisted he was quitting. He asked what the title would mean to his father if he only earned it by betraying me. If this was the price of the win, he would rather burn the title than take it.

It should have landed as kindness. Instead, it was venom. I felt it coursing through my veins in real time. My mother and I can't lose our relationship for nothing. He better get over it.

"Not your choice to make, fighter. I have destroyed every relationship in my life for you. You better fight, and you better win. Sure cost me enough."

I still hate him. But I know, somehow, he got the message.

I dismantled the drones. I couldn't destroy them. Literally, I don't have the right equipment. The control chips? Those I could have destroyed. I didn't. I locked them in my secret vault. Somewhere deep in me, I wish I could crawl in there with them and stay hidden.

Just for a while or forever... one of the two.

Diary Entry # 19 – The Breaking Point

A.T. 269, Month 1, Day 36 (Tulan Standard Time)

Things have been... normal. Is this what passes for normal? I committed what some call treason, Dad's facing a tribunal, Mom won't look me in the eye. She hasn't said a word to me since I called her that. The only person I ever trusted is still avoiding me like I'm contagious. That feels about right.

Mom hates me, but she's still doing her overlording duties. I know she told the teachers to keep an eye on me. They hover. One followed me to the bathroom and waited outside the stall. I can't even grab a pencil without someone tracking the motion like it's a threat. I'd hate it if home wasn't so quiet. Dad left for his tribunal two days ago. Home is silent.

No release. No models. No experiments. No lab. I'm surprised they still let me read books. Better be careful. I might get ideas.

I spend every free second in the library now. If I can't build something, I can learn something. Plan something. Think beyond the walls they've boxed me into. They can't keep me down forever. They might not have to.

Today broke me.

Ms. Halin kicked me out of the library at lunch. I wasn't supposed to be in there. Fine. I didn't want to deal with recess and she knew. She felt bad, I could tell, but she couldn't override the Headmistress. Or the Queen. I warned her it would be a problem.

I don't even remember the walk from the library to the field. By the time I hit the edge of the grass, I was crying. Not a tear or two. A full-blown breakdown. No Alley to pull me out of it. He hasn't come back. Not really. He's still out there, running himself into the ground. I'm not there to stop his inevitable fall off a cliff.

I hate how worried I am. I'm supposed to hate him… right?

I found a quiet patch under a tree. Out of sight. Or so I thought.

"I heard you and your boyfriend broke up."

Sarah. Of course it was Sarah. God's punishing me now. I probably earned that one.

"You deserve better than him anyway," she added, like she was giving sisterly advice. Like we were friends.

I tried to ignore her. I really did. She kept going. Alley's dumb. Just muscle. A pretty face. No depth. I used every deep-breathing technique Dad ever taught me not to launch her across the field.

Just when I thought it was over, her imp overlord Stroud showed up. He lobbed a handful of mud on us. Thick, wet, and rancid, like he mixed it with dung. Some of it caught Sarah too. She shrieked and stormed off, muttering about keeping her pet on a leash.

Most of it hit me. Right across my coat. Dr. Childs' lab coat.

"What is his problem?" I whispered. Not to anyone. Not really.

Vault Diary - Hypothesis Oblivion

I didn't wait for an answer. Just walked away.

I found another spot. Wiped my sleeves. Tried to bury myself in a book.

An even larger splatter of mud hit right across the page. My notes and calculations reduced to smears of sludge.

"Sorry. Maybe try somewhere a little further away."

Stroud laughed. I wanted to scream. Or cry. Or break something.

Instead… I obeyed. I was already on thin ice. What choice did I have?

I found a patch behind the equipment shed. Quiet. Out of sight.

A minute before recess ended, Stroud gave me his final present: a whole bucket of his latest brew. Cold, wet mud, whatever that smelly mixture was, poured from above. Soaked me. Head to boots. Stroud howled. He smeared the mud into my scalp like shampoo.

He knew I couldn't fight back. That I wouldn't.

He miscalculated.

I slapped him. Hard. Went to do it again. He was ready. Caught my hand. Hit me back.

I hit the ground. His friends jumped in, mostly jeering as they shoved me about. Alley always told me never to fight angry, and boy did I not listen. No follow-through, bad stance; no wonder I tanked every hit. I gave him two pathetic slaps. He gave me a full-strength right hook across the cheek. I felt every thought in my head jolt when I hit the ground. I could hear Alley screaming in my skull: *Don't let him pin you.* I scrambled up, only to find the next fight had already started. It was a lot more one-sided.

Alley. He appeared out of nowhere.

Moved like a weapon. Precise. Relentless. Stroud never stood a chance. Stroud's friends got tagged once and ran. Alley let them go.

Stroud was a marked man. Alley wasn't holding back. Not this time.

It took me five seconds too long to realize Alley wasn't going to stop. Stroud couldn't defend himself anymore, but every time Stroud started to back off he glanced at me, and Alley punched him again.

"Stop it! I started the fight! I started the fight!" I yelled. He didn't care. I had to throw myself on top of Stroud, covering him with my body, to make it end. What scared me most when he finally stopped was the look in his eyes. He would have killed him. I saw it. He knew it. He looked at me, breathing hard.

I saw Alley—the moment he came back. Not the crazed lunatic who'd been training for months, but my friend. The horror in his eyes as he looked at me and Stroud's limp body said it all. He told me to tell the truth. That he'd back me up. That he had to talk to his mom. To tell Aunt Cristal he was sorry. He didn't say what for. He didn't say anything else after that, except goodbye. It felt final.

I almost called out. Just his name. Just once. The words caught in my throat.

By the time the adults showed up, he was already gone.

I don't know if I'll ever see him again. I hope I do. I'll still be mad, but...

Our story can't end like this.

The Tournament

Diary Entry # 20 – He Loves Me. I Think.

A.T. 269, Month 1, Day 43 (Tulan Standard Time)

She was furious at first. Gave me the full lecture: *"You cannot just pick fights, Maria. Do you want to end up in an alternative school like Alley?"*

I don't even know where the response came from. *"If that makes me half the person he is, sign me up."*

I actually said that? I don't regret it. I don't get it. He set me up. He betrayed me. He left me to take the fall. Why would I say that? I plead temporary insanity. Best defense I have—temporary but very persistent. It came out before I had time to think. Come to think of it, that's the first thing she's said to me… fitting.

Before I could even begin to process that, Alley burst in.

The door practically cracked on its hinges. I think Mom forgot how to speak for twenty full seconds. He stood there, panting, tense like a bowstring. Did he run home and back after the fight? I think he did. It took him twelve seconds to catch his breath.

"Mistress Maze, please don't punish her. This was my fault."

"Mistress Maze." He actually called her Mistress Maze. I think he bowed. I know he was dry-heaving internally the whole time doing it. I'm dry-heaving just thinking about it.

He explained everything. Stroud stole his journal. Found out I was already on thin ice. When Alley confronted him,

Stroud threatened to stir up trouble for me if he turned him in. Alley said Stroud knew I was one of his *buttons*. Hurting me was just payback. A warning. A flaunt.

He insisted none of it was my fault. Mom couldn't absolve me completely. In truth, neither could I.

Turns out she already knew about the journal—Stroud stole Alley's passcode from her office to break into his locker.

Stroud is suspended. I'm grounded another week. That means I'll be grounded during the tournament.

As for Alley? Mom said she's trying to find a reason not to expel him. He's lucky he's too young to be arrested for assault, and he was two punches away from being charged with murder. No age limit on that.

Then she added, almost like it hurt to say: *"I know you were defending my daughter, Alejandro. I will remember that too."*

She told him to go home. He'll have a penalty by the end of the week. In the meantime, no more one-class-a-day vanishing acts. He'd better be in class tomorrow. Every class.

His request to transfer classes? Denied.

At the door, she gave him a quiet thank-you. *"Your father would be proud of your intentions, but you have to learn control."*

How did she know that's what this was all about? I perked up for a second, hoping he'd take solace. He didn't. He left without another word.

Mom said we'd talk later. She sent me to bed and said she'd see what she could do with Dr. Childs' coat.

The answer? Nothing. It's ruined. Whatever Stroud mixed that mud with started breaking down the fabric.

So here I am. That was more than a week ago. I'm still confused. Mom might kill me if she finds out I stopped writing in my diary for so long. I just didn't know what to say. Hope the family forgives me for not doing the whole family history thing. Still not sure why my diary's supposed to matter anyway.

Stop distracting yourself, Maria. Focus. Alley. What do I do with Alley? I can't keep dodging this question. He has made it easy, though. He kept skipping classes for another week. Mom had to threaten to expel him if he missed any more classes, right in front of Aunt Linda. He agreed to return tomorrow. I have to know what my plan is.

I know I should ditch him. He betrayed me. That part's clear. I should ditch him, but I don't want to. I don't know, or maybe don't want to know, why.

Okay. Stop.

What do I know, objectively? He defended me. This lapse in judgment aside, he's always had my back. He made a mistake and is trying to fix it. He just stinks at it. In the end, he loves me.

Wait, did I just say that?

I mean, the facts support it. So... yes.

I guess that's objectively true.

Oh no! Given the facts, I think I... objectively love him too.

Strangely, that makes it easier. He gets that obnoxious, illogical grace reserved for loved people.

He loves me. I love him. He regrets what he did. He came back. He's still here.

Alley, if you ever read this... I'll have to kill you. For real. Can't let you figure that "I love you" part out. Too dangerous.

Diary Update:

Alley's officially disqualified from the Tournament. Tomorrow... I guess I need to remember how to be a friend. He'll need one. I know he'll be devastated. I'll forget this whole thing just for tomorrow.

I'll finish his torture later.

Diary Entry # 21 – A Working Treaty

A.T. 269, Month 1, Day 59 (Alphaeus Standard Time)

It's been a different kind of time.

Alley wasn't crushed about being disqualified. I think it was a relief for him. Given everything that happened, all he wanted was to wipe the slate clean. The next tournament is in two years. He's already started training.

Lorenz-I took Alley's spot in the tournament. Getting him on board was the hardest part. He didn't feel like he had earned it. Technically, he was the alternate, placed second in qualifiers, but he didn't think that was enough. Alley got him to come around.

Mom gave Alley in-school suspension. She said he couldn't afford any more time away. Honestly, I think she was just trying to protect him.

Alley finally apologized to me. Not just a vague "sorry," a real one.

He said he was most ashamed of taking advantage of my mind.

"I used you because you cared."

He's devastated, completely having an identity crisis. It makes torturing him a little complicated. His mom grounded him for two months but gave him an exception to attend the tournament. She thought it was punishment, watching others compete when it could have been him. For him, it wasn't punishment. He got to support Lorenz-I, and that was enough.

He asked if there was any chance my mom would let me go. To my absolute shock, she said yes.

Alley asked for my permission to let Lorenz-I use the training braces and support materials I built. Turns out, he had already let him use them without asking. It wasn't until the day before the tournament that it even hit him that I might have had a problem with that.

I let it go. I think he really believes he's my brother, that everything of mine is his. He hasn't earned it yet, but he's getting there.

Lorenz-I was really grateful. Humble. Quiet, but focused. A very different kind of fighter than Alley. More precise. More methodical. Still dangerous. Lorenz-I and Alley trained after school on our land every day. I watched.

It was strange, seeing Alley teach someone else using everything I helped him build.

It wasn't quite as satisfying as watching Alley use it himself, but it was close.

Lorenz-I won. He won the whole tournament.

I still can't believe how loud we were shouting in the stands when he landed the final blow in the battle royale. We were on our feet, screaming like lunatics.

Afterward, he limped over to Alley and collapsed into his arms. We took him straight to the medical bay. As bad as he looked, bruised, beaten, half-dragging one leg, I couldn't help thinking, why would anyone want to win this tournament?

Still, we did. Not the win Alley wanted. Not the path I thought I'd take.

Enough though, definitely enough.

Story 004: Containment Failure

Much of science is controlled destruction. Creation demands failure, millions of them, for every success. That's one of the reasons I believe in God. To pursue science means accepting destruction as part of the process, to wield entropy with a curious mind and a reckless kind of trust. Ethics helps determine who and what must pay for those failures. Unfortunately, sometimes even ethics fail. It's a hard lesson. I was much too young when I learned it.

Diary Entry # 22 – Back in the Lab

A.T. 269, Month 2, Day 35 (Tulan Standard Time)

I'm finally off punishment. It took forever. Alley better never pull something like that again. I may actually have to kick him off the friend list.

Wait a minute. Alley *is* the friend list. That makes him my best friend. I mean, I guess by default. Maybe I should get a pen pal or something just so Alley can have some competition. (Who am I kidding? He wouldn't care.)

Anyway, new project time. I've started working on energy resonance enhancement. Talk about *fascinating*. Did you know most of the devices we use on the farm operate at around 76% efficiency?

Seventy-six!

I think I've figured out a method to use resonance modulation to increase efficiency, cut fuel use by more than half, and double productivity. I'm doing this through a mix of a rebuilt engine and a modification to the harvester design. I already built a prototype engine for it. I still can't believe Mom never caught me sneaking out to the storage shed. I gutted one of the old harvesters for parts. It hadn't run in years, so I figured no one would miss it, except maybe the mice nesting inside.

The experiment is coming up. This time, I went through all the safeguards. All of them. Twice. I even showed Mom and got on a call with Dr. Childs to confirm everything. He asked a few questions I hadn't thought of, which is why I'm glad I checked. Final verdict: everything is a go. My first full showcase experiment. The protocols are a doldrum, but I'll take anything that keeps Alley out of the hospital.

Today was the demonstration. Alley, Mom, and a representative from the Agricultural Board came to watch.

I ran the harvester through a ten-by-ten section of the field using ten milliliters of fuel in twenty-five minutes. That's about a quarter of the usual fuel for that size plot. Unheard of. It worked perfectly. I am literally trembling. This is amazing!

Come to think of it, I just got excited about running a harvester, the most boring piece of farm equipment there is. You just sit on it and drive. Science really *can* make anything fun.

Mom was elated. Alley looked impressed, and the official said the board would definitely want to hear more. I have to admit, it feels really good to be building again, doing something that helps. Mom's been so stressed about the harvest this year. Last year wasn't great, and we mostly survived on tuition from Rain Province families who send their kids to school here.

Her workers' kids go for free, which makes up about 70% of the student body, and she doesn't want to raise tuition. The other 30%, mostly from Rain Province, fund the entire operation. Raising their tuition would drive them away, and she's trying to avoid that.

Vault Diary - Hypothesis Oblivion

I hope this helps.

She even offered to help me with the write-up. We start tomorrow. That's probably the first real smile I've seen from her in weeks. It was a good day.

Good night for now, diary.

Containment Failure

Diary Entry # 23 – The Fire

A.T. 269, Month 2, Day 36 (Tulan Standard Time)

I should have known it was too good to last. I swear my life is nothing but a nonstop trudge through a field of landmines. Strap in.

I woke up to the sound of alarms echoing across the cornfield. I knew exactly where it was coming from.

The shed. The storage shed where I kept the prototype.

I ran.

There's nothing like hearing a blaring alarm while you're surrounded by nothing but corn stalks. Endless, towering corn stalks. You feel so small, so lost, so close to something terrible, like a feral beast will emerge from the stalks to devour you. To be fair, that isn't far from the truth of the night.

When I got to the shed, the prototype was on fire. So was half the stored corn.

It's not possible. I shut the engine down before I left last night. Disconnected everything. Removed the harvester prototype engine. I even took the power core upstairs to my attic lab.

Mom went full Inquisitor mode the second she arrived, after we got the fire out. The cause is a mystery. The results are not. We lost 25% of the crop.

Vault Diary - Hypothesis Oblivion

My modified engine, or what's left of it, spilled toxic chemicals into the ground. We have to neutralize it, or we could lose the entire field for years.

Mom is on the comm with Dad, furious. She thinks my experiment caused the fire. I tried to explain, tried to tell her the engine was shut down, that I had taken every precaution. But the evidence is bad. Really bad. The center of the explosion was right where my engine sat. What's left of it is torn to ribbons.

She won't even listen to me. I told her it's impossible. I showed her my schematics and went over the science of combustion. It's like explaining calculus to a toddler. I am empirically, mathematically innocent. It doesn't matter.

I'm banned. Again. No more energy research. No more experiments. Just like that. Not for the destruction. No, I'm banned for running into the fire. She yelled at me for running into the fire.

I get it. Apparently, I have moderate smoke inhalation and some bruised ribs from a support beam that collapsed while I was in there. I guess I forgot to mention a support beam snapped and swung right into my ribs.

I was trying to protect the harvest. I put the fire out on the corn. It didn't help. The remaining crop in that section has to be destroyed anyway because of the contamination.

So I risked everything and saved nothing.

It still doesn't make sense. Engines don't explode without power. Mine had no core, no fuel, no live current. So how did it blow? I've gone over my schematics five times. Six. I can't find the fault.

The worst part is that one of the workers, who was out early prepping another section, is in the hospital. Critical condition. He can't talk. Can't write. Struggling to breathe.

Mom is with him now. She's covering his care. She didn't even yell when she left, just looked tired.

I'm at home with Alley and Aunt Linda. Alley's trying to stop me from tearing through blueprints again like I'll find absolution buried in page six. He says every time I touch something like this, I leave chaos behind when I don't think it through. He's probably right.

I can't just do nothing. I have to help Mom. I know I didn't do it this time. I have to prove it. I have all my schematics laid out in front of me. Everything.

I just can't find where or how this is possible.

Diary Entry # 24 – The Back Room

A.T. 269, Month 2, Day 37 (Tulan Standard Time)

Short entry today. I actually have a role to play in recon-struction, by design. Mom put me in charge of the chemical cleanup. Thank goodness she gave me something. Maybe she's trying to give me a controlled way to help without risking another explosion. Maybe she's starting to get me.

Doubtful. But a girl can dream.

I've been learning a lot about botany and biochemistry. I think I can decontaminate the area. The storage shed is a lost cause and will have to be rebuilt, but the cleanup is doable.

Honestly, it's not that different from working the harvest, except nothing you pick is going to be eaten, or at least not by people. The microbe barns will be stocked for ages. Everything is going to be destroyed, buried, processed, or broken down by microorganisms. None of it is of much use.

The empty storage room in the back was the only part not damaged. We're going to lose about 5% of our usable land for the next two years. To compensate, I need to increase the profitability of the rest. That means improving yield per area.

While researching fertilizer strategies, I found some successful methods used in other parts of Tula and on Rolvair VII, including cross-pollination techniques, mineral enhancement, and timing cycles.

It's not my invention. I'm not building anything new, Mom. Just using what's already available. Perfectly safe.

I showed Alley the plan and asked if he would help me get the materials. There's no way I could carry it all alone. He agreed. He said he owed me for the tournament, but next time he's charging. Yeah, right. He's literally never said no. Besides, he better not tell me no. I can guilt with the best of them.

The good news is that the chemical agents we need are mostly byproducts. A few companies in Liviton were happy to part with them. Ecstatic, actually. Alley helped me load everything into the family velo. I sat in the back with the canisters and held them during the trip. I have never been so nauseous after a ride in my life.

The ruined storage shed is my makeshift lab for now. I brought down tables and chairs to do the chemical mixing. I told Mom, and she seems okay with it.

"At least it's safe," she said.

One strange thing, though. When I got back to the shed tonight, some of my materials had been moved. I could have sworn I left the canisters stacked against the entry to the back storage room. I'm sure I did. I figured nobody needed to get back there anyway. When I came back, the storage room door was exposed.

It was still closed, but no longer blocked. I guess Alley moved the canisters before he left. Why? Maybe to keep the storage room exit open, so we could use the back room?

It doesn't make sense. The whole building is basically condemned.

That room isn't big enough for mixing.

Diary Entry # 25 – White Dust and Shadows

A.T. 269, Month 2, Day 38 (Tulan Standard Time)

Someone has been living in the back room of the storage shed. I'm sure of it. I went out to the lab last night, and I know I heard someone in there. Moving. Breathing. I didn't check the rooms, though. I was there by myself. I'm crazy, not stupid. I just locked all the doors and left.

I told Mom this morning. There was no sign of anyone. She said I'm just making it up to distract from the idea that my prototype started the fire. I didn't respond. I've barely spoken to her since, and she doesn't get why. She insists she doesn't blame me, like that's the problem. How does she not see?

What really hurts is that she thinks I would lie like that. We don't lie, not in this family. I've had plenty of chances to lie my way out of trouble, but I never took them. That's not who we are. When I reminded her of my record and my history of telling the truth, she wouldn't hear it. She insists the shed is empty, that there's no evidence of an intruder, no signs of tampering.

Fine. I'll prove it.

Alley and I finished mixing the fertilizer right after school and stored it in the back room. The extra I placed in the storage room.

Vault Diary - Hypothesis Oblivion

If someone is staying there, they'll get a very smelly surprise next time they sneak in. I told Alley about the intruder, and he insisted on staying at my house tonight.

We spread the fertilizer over the crop after sundown, one full coat to last the season. We won't need another round for two months, which means no one has any reason to go near the shed again. Perfect.

Last thing we did before coming in? We set the trap.

The power systems were fried during the fire, and a portable camera is too easy to destroy or rig. I can't set up much without a lab. My solution: five bags of flour. White dust, spread across the entire storage room. Every inch. Whoever has been sneaking in is going to leave tracks.

This time, I'll have proof.

Alley and I went back to the guest room and set up a watch. We've been watching the shed for hours. I'll transcribe this later.

Nothing yet. I bet whoever it is waits for the cover of darkness.

Wait. Someone's there. Now she'll believe me.

I can't see his face yet, but he's tall. About five ten. Definitely Kameonic.

Carrying a torch into a barn full of fertili—

Diary Entry # 26 – The Blast

A.T. 269, Month 2, Day 39 (Tulan Standard Time)

"If Alley dies, Cristal Maze, I swear to God, I will kill you."

My aunt said it. Right in front of my mother. And my father. Neither of them said anything. She left without another word. I've never seen her so enraged and destroyed at the same time. I couldn't tell if she was going to wring Mom's neck or collapse into her arms. Uncle Quince came to see me but said nothing to either one.

The intruder's name was Rickshaw Jenkave. He left Mom's service three years ago to start his own farm. He lost it and has been homeless ever since. Turns out he's been sleeping in the back room of the storage shed for months. He stole a key and had a copy made.

The worker, who just stepped down from critical condition this afternoon, confirmed what I didn't want to believe. The engine was active the night of the fire. When he told Mom, it explained everything. How could I not see it before? I never considered that someone might put a power core into my engine. The shed was supposed to be abandoned.

Rickshaw must have put a standard power core into my prototype engine. I didn't design it for that. The control systems would have failed immediately, causing a catastrophic meltdown. He didn't mean to destroy the shed. There was a cold snap that night. He just wanted to be warm. You're not supposed to use those engines for warmth, but people do it.

When it overloaded, he panicked and ran.

Rickshaw took the worst of it. He didn't make it. My flour trap, the one I was so proud of, became microscopic shrapnel in the blast.

I tried to warn Alley. Told him to stay back. For once, he did the math faster than I did.

The last thing I heard was him yelling, "Get out of there!"

I got a broken arm. By my estimate, the shockwave slammed me into the house wall with an impact speed of fifteen miles per hour. Alley wasn't so lucky. He has a massive concussion and hasn't woken up.

So I have a literal fatality, my best friend is in a coma, and I broke my own arm. I made everything worse. Again. Nothing could make this worse, right?

Wrong again.

Turns out the fertilizer I synthesized was contaminated. One of the byproducts in it reacted with the base compound, dangerously, once exposed to heat and pressure.

That's what triggered the secondary explosion. I gave the Army Explosives Division my full recipe, every source, every note. They interrogated me for over an hour. My dad sat behind me the whole time.

When it was over, one of the privates muttered, "Stick to baking cakes, kid."

A week ago, I would have gone off. If Alley were here, I know he would have. I just sat there. Dad told the private to watch himself. I can't put into words how much I appreciated Dad at that moment. Still, I don't know.

Maybe he's right.
Maybe I should just stop.

Vault Diary - Hypothesis Oblivion

Diary Entry # 27 – Exclusion Zone

A.T. 269, Month 2, Day 47 (Tulan Standard Time)

I haven't seen Alley, Aunt Linda, or Uncle Quince in almost a week. I know Alley was discharged from the hospital right before the weekend. I'm just glad he's alive. I cried myself to sleep for three days.

It's not just about Alley. My mom and Aunt Linda have been best friends since they were kids. I have actual aunts, but I don't see them a quarter as much as I see Aunt Linda. She's one of the few people who gets me.

Uncle Quince is the father I sometimes wish I had. (If you ever read this, you're okay, Dad. Frankly, if you're reading this, this isn't even the worst thing you'll see me say about you. So I digress.)

The problem is that I didn't just ruin my own life. I possibly ruined Mom's, Dad's, Uncle Quince's, and Aunt Linda's. I almost killed Alley.

I did kill Mr. Jenkave. He wasn't a bad man. He used to be so kind. Always cleared the school field first so we had room to play, with Mom yelling at him the whole time. The school-yard probably took a whole day to clear and was likely the least profitable section, but he still did it.

I wonder when he saw me last if he knew he was talking to his executioner.

Mom feels horrible. She blames herself. Apparently, Mr. Jenkave asked for his old job back this year and last year but came too late, after hiring season.

I overheard her telling Dad, "If I had just helped him, none of this would have happened."

His family came down to Tula for the funeral. He didn't own a grave, so Mom cleared space for him on the family plot. He had a job. He was working, trying to provide for his family. Now they don't have him.

Mom's doing what she can to help them transition. His family has been surprisingly okay with everything. They're not yelling or blaming us. They're not saying we killed their husband, father, or provider. They're just quiet.

It should be comforting. It isn't.
Why are they so nonchalant?
Maybe they don't want us to see them cry. I probably wouldn't, either.

The entire storage shed was destroyed in the blast. I've gone out every day since, clearing the crop. It has to be shipped to Pyrosia IV to be incinerated. We lost an entire crop. Mom told me we have the money, that I shouldn't worry about our survival, that this isn't a problem for me. I just hate that I've made her work harder.

I overheard that she's increasing school enrollment, charging her staff 2% of their income for tuition. It's nothing compared to what regular students pay. Even so, I hate that it's my fault.

Dad tried to cheer me up. He said the Lentil Company, the ones we got the contaminated chemicals from, used us to dump their waste and lied about the mixture. Two of their executives are on their way to Chamber Prison on Kameon Centrum. He said it wasn't my fault. He's wrong.

Dad's always been fine with stretching the truth, unlike Mom. I know he's just trying to protect me. I appreciate that, but I'm done.

I've started burning all of my biochemistry notes, my science journals, all of it.

Everything that was useful has already been written up. I sent Dr. Childs a copy of the modified harvester schematics and my final notes before I burned them. Since the engine didn't cause the fire, maybe he can give the design to someone else. I spent the last week learning how to write patents. I wrote the patent for my engine and transferred ownership to Mr. Jenkave's widow. Maybe someone else can finish what I started, because it won't be me. Whatever's earned, she should have it. She paid enough for it.

As for me, I can't do this anymore.

Diary Entry # 28 – Mended Robes

A.T. 269, Month 2, Day 53 (Tulan Standard Time)

Apparently, I'm not supposed to hear death threats.

Aunt Linda came by with Alley and Uncle Quince today. I'll admit, I threw myself at her mercy. Full-on groveling before her majesty. She met it with dry amusement until I asked her not to take it out on Mom. I told her everything was my fault, that I was the one who stored the fertilizer in the shed and came up with the flour trap. I set everything in motion.

Her reaction was pure shock. Uncle Quince knelt beside me and wrapped an arm around my shoulders. "Moms can get a little psychotic when their kids are hurt," he said. It was like he was trying to find the best word, and "psychotic" was the most tame one. Mom and Aunt Linda agreed. Mom admitted she would have made the same threat if Alley and I had switched places. Then came the apologies and the hug, like their last interaction hadn't nearly escalated into a silent duel at dawn.

Aunt Linda said I wasn't supposed to hear that. She apologized to me. Why? I nearly killed her kid. Seriously. I don't get adults.

Alley pulled me upstairs after that, into the attic. His head still has a nasty knot, but he brushed it off like it was nothing. He asked what we were getting into today, but I told him no more fieldwork. I had tried to keep helping, but the doctor banned me from it. When he asked what I was working on, I told him: burning my last energy journals.

He called me melodramatic, and yeah… maybe he's right. Then he asked why I would destroy one of the most interesting things about myself. Why did he even have to ask? He was standing right there, living proof of everything that went wrong. I told him we could walk to the family grove if he needed to see a reason.

He didn't have an answer for that. He just hugged me. A real hug. Long, quiet, steady. I don't know how long he held me, but I needed every second.

He asked me not to give up my best selling point over one little explosion. I told him he couldn't change my mind. He didn't press further, just muttered that I'd ruined his surprise.

Turns out he got me a new aqua blue lab coat. He said he agreed with Dr. Childs, it's a good look on me. I told him maybe I'd just wear it while doing model design. He shrugged and said, "Whatever keeps my money from being wasted." Classic Alley. Stingy with his imaginary investments.

I've already got a new model to build. Life will go back to what it was. I keep telling myself that. Over and over. Maybe if I say it enough times, it'll be true.

Who am I kidding, they're kind of boring. There's nothing to explore, nothing to discover. I know what works. There's no guesswork. No risk.

Later that night, Mom came up to the attic. First words out of her mouth? "What's this I hear about you giving up science?" Did Alley... tell my mother? Wow... snitch. Honestly, I thought she'd be happy about it when she found out. She was the one warning me about the dangers. I told her she'd been right all along.

She looked tired, not triumphant. When I mentioned giving up energy and chemistry, I half-joked about switching to biology. That earned a quick "no thank you." I told her the trash was coming soon and she could toss my astrophysics books. I said I'd hang up the lab coat. Maybe just wear it when Alley visits. Model work isn't real science anyway, no discovery, no risk.

She didn't argue. She just took the books and stacked them neatly in the corner. "You might need them again one day," she said. I didn't watch her leave, but she left me something on the way out that I didn't notice until just now.

Right before I sat down to write this, I found it sitting on my bed. A book, wrapped in Dr. Childs' old lab coat—my robes perfectly restored. I still don't know how she managed that one. Alley's new coat was folded next to it. The book was a treatise on transmission carrier waves, something I hadn't studied yet. There was a note on top, in Mom's handwriting: "It's safe. Maybe start there."

When I picked up Dr. Childs' coat to hang it up, I found more underneath. A small toolkit, a group of transmitters, and the safety protocol manual Dr. Childs gave me months ago. On top of all that was a folded piece of paper with one sentence, handwritten:

"You're going to need your lab coat."

It meant a lot that she tried. It really did.

Maybe just this one thing. Maybe I'll try. How much trouble could I get into with this?

I put on Alley's coat and opened the treatise.

Story 005: The Xaolin

My childhood ended on A.T. 269, Month 4, Day 4, at 2:05 A.M. Eleven years and five months old. I guess some last longer. I would have mourned, but I was more concerned with whether I'd see another sunrise. The Xaolin took so much from me. I hated them for so long, feared them for so much longer. I never considered what they gave me. I am who I am because of the evil they brought.

So... thank you, demons who tried to steal my soul. You taught me to keep my guard up. Always have a safe space, even if it can only be the depths of my mind.

Diary Entry # 29 – Static

A.T. 269, Month 4, Day 01 (Tulan Standard Time)

The school year ended today.

I am so excited. A few weeks of not having to deal with Stroud? Bliss. I might actually enjoy being outside again.

I'll give this communications thing credit, it's fascinating. I've started specializing in covert transmissions. Alley and I have been having a blast. We even built a planet-wide communicator. Talking to him from the other side of the world? Awesome. I haven't made anything that can clear the atmosphere yet, but I've got a sketched design for a micro-interstellar comm scanner.

Alley came over after school. I was on cloud nine. Alley… not so much.

All my final marks came back glowing. My teacher even made a note about me "exceeding known educational baselines." I think that's her way of saying I broke the grading curve.

Alley, though, said physics took him down. He said he never should have taken it in the first place. I told him he just wanted an excuse to spend more evenings here studying. He didn't deny it.

My comm studies have made me a lot better at computers. It's such a fun subject. It feels like standing on the shoulders of giants. Everything I build is based on someone else's code, someone else's logic. Yet, I have total control. I love that.

I showed Alley my comm scanner. It was fun at first, just cycling through local channels and picking up stray transmissions. We heard a couple of kids talking about snacks, a pair of siblings yelling at each other, and one guy singing off-key to a song he clearly didn't know the lyrics to.

Then it got weird. We found a cluster of signals that were clearly encrypted.

That's when I pulled up the decryption program I've been writing. Dad gave me some old decryption keys from abandoned systems. They're useless on their own, but my program stitches fragments together to build new language keys. It's still in the early phases, but it decoded a fragment.

And the fragment? Names.
My name.

Cristal Maze.
Brooks Roamai.
Perrian Tnerret.
Melissa Cramer.
John Cramer.

At first I thought maybe it was a coincidence, until the next set of transmissions produced another fragment with my full name and location. I let the computer keep running and bolted to get Mom.

I showed her what the scanner was picking up.
She didn't ask questions. Didn't blink. She was trembling.

She just shut the whole system down, told me to go to my room, and called Aunt Linda. No explanation. No feedback. Just silence. Before she left, she addressed me.

"Stop working on comm projects. We'll talk when I get back."

Something is wrong. She doesn't sound angry. She sounds worried, panicked. I don't know what scares me more, her fear or my questions. I know she has answers. It's always the worst when she won't share them. That's when I know the truth is worse than anything I can imagine.

Diary Entry # 30 – Target List

A.T. 269, Month 4, Day 02 (Tulan Standard Time)

Dad called us via subspace video. A full mission briefing.

Every listed target was there. Names and faces I'd only ever heard in passing filled the screen. Executive General Perrian, running the investigation and trying, badly, to console his wife. Executive General Towelain, head of Special Operations. And at the top of it all, Supreme Commander Cramer and his wife, who looked ready to kill the entire threat single-handedly. If she was scared, none of it showed.

The Commander let my father report the facts himself. Only now does it dawn on me that he might have done that for me. He's not quite Uncle John, but he's been a family friend for as long as I can remember.

Dad confirmed that the message I intercepted was a list of targets. The army has been working hard to rein in Xaolin aggression. Their strike tactics relied on using dark-space nebulae for cover during covert attacks. That was why Dad had to come work on the research station above Tula. With recent advancements, dark-space strikes aren't really an option for them anymore. They've already killed Dr. Childs—another body on my list of casualties. Dad paused a moment too late.

They had to stop the call. I couldn't stop bawling. Mom wiped my eyes like she was smoothing wood with sandpaper. No time to cry now. She stared at me, shouted at me with her voice, with a static burst. The voice said, "Hush!" The static burst said, "It's not your fault, Maria." She meant it to make me feel better.

Why did it feel like the first lie she ever told me? Maybe because she did flinch this time.

Dad insisted it isn't just about my dark-space collector. Apparently, Dr. Childs modified it into an autonomous sentry drone and leaked the tech to the Chan. Both Perrian and Towelain groaned. Under his breath, Perrian muttered, "Traitor."

Dad assured us the Xaolin must be working for someone, someone with strong opinions about the recent treaty the Kameonic Army reached with the Chan. It's just a non-aggression pact. Why would the Xaolin care at all?

I guess the truth is, they don't. They never care. They're assassins. They get a name, a file, and a payout. Then they make someone disappear.

Guess my name's up.

Dad said the Xaolin have already made moves, targeting top military brass and their families. Just as telling as who's on the list is who isn't. Strangely, the generals who opposed the treaty seem to have been spared.

Dad didn't mince words. He said it's too early to know how serious this operation is. Is it a pressure campaign, or just someone trying to scare us? Either way, it's working. The army's not taking chances. They're working their sources now, trying to find out if any of the names have a hit out on them. Towelain and Perrian are responsible for our safety but insist we stay put until they have better information.

I still can't believe anyone would want to kill me. For what? What would that even accomplish? It has to be wrong. Right?

Mom taught me a symbol. It looked like two infinity signs, one horizontal and one vertical, with an arrow pointing away from the center.

She said if I ever see that symbol: run.

Don't look back.
Don't wait for her.
Don't try to understand.
Just run.

Find someone you trust with your life, because your life will be in their hands.

I hope they're overreacting. They have to be overreacting.

Today was… semi-normal. At least, on the surface. Alley's been staying with us. He was there for the symbol lesson. He already knew it.

He's been quiet today. On edge. He's carrying a single-edge blade now, and he showed me how to use a shield arm cannon. I'd only ever seen those on active duty soldiers and Dad.

Now I have to learn to aim one. These things weigh a ton. I can barely lift it, let alone aim it. Alley said he has some exercises to strengthen my forearms. I need them. My highest score after three hours of training was a 6. I need to score a 22. I don't want to. I hate violence.

I left science to stop the danger, to stop causing problems. Danger keeps finding me anyway.

Maybe nothing will happen.
Please let nothing happen.

Diary Entry # 31 – The Night It Happened

A.T. 269, Month 4, Day 04 (Tulan Standard Time)

I… I… I… I can't.
I don't know where to begin.

My knight has fallen.
That's the best way I can say it, I guess. Maybe not the most intellectual phrasing, but right now my brain doesn't work.

Alley spent half the day figuring out which weapon I'd be most effective with, something I could actually use without months of training. Double-stick won out, not because it was easy, but because somehow… I already knew how to move with them. He said I had "innate dual-sync." Whatever that means.

I hate to say it, but I think Alley enjoyed this crisis. He smiled while training me. We laughed. I'd be lying if I said I didn't enjoy it too. Fighting and fencing are apparently "adjacent," and Dad did give me fencing lessons when I was younger. Now I wish I had never given it up. If I survive this, I'll train every day.

Tonight, we locked up. That said, you can't tell me we're under threat and not expect me to science. I built an early warning system. It wasn't fancy, just basic motion sensors linked to my comm unit. It worked.

Too late. They were inside before we woke up.

Vault Diary - Hypothesis Oblivion

I opened my eyes to what should have been my final vision. A man I've never seen was standing over me with a sickle blade at my throat, cold, sharp. The edge was stained red with the blood of a former victim, hungry for a fresh coat. I froze. I couldn't scream. I couldn't think. I wish my Aquian abilities were awake. I could've shocked him, maybe.

It wasn't me who saved me.

Alley dove over my bed and shouted something I couldn't understand, something that sounded like "old Tulan" or "ancient Magician" language. He tackled the attacker and beat him until he didn't get up again.

Alley's shout tore through the house like a cannon blast. Then chaos. The whole house felt like a war zone. Fighters everywhere. Alley kept me close. Mom was in full battle mode.

They moved like they were built for it.

"Get her out," my mother shouted, scrambling against two assailants. I just kept getting in the way. Every time I tried to help, someone had to save me. I felt useless. No. I was useless.

I don't fight. I don't shoot. I can barely aim. So I did the only thing I could do. Chemistry.

I scrambled into the laundry room and jimmied together some smoke bombs with household cleaners, pressurizers, and sealant caps. I burned my fingers on the third one. It hissed when I sealed it; it was live. I had three seconds.

I screamed outside Mom's door. She came running. I had to get it in there. Throw it, or die trying.

I chucked the device, slammed the door, and jammed it shut.

Two seconds later, pop. Smoke. Thin wisps crawled under the door. Sunrise before they recover… if they recover. I didn't have time to think about that.

We sprinted to find Alley. He was surrounded, barely holding on. Mom pulled him out while I tossed another smoke bomb to buy us cover. We bolted through the cornfield and into the woods.

She'd already moved the velo. We're officially on the run.

We have nothing but what we carried:

>One fully charged velo.
>A weapons kit.
>My comm scanner and code processor.
>Ourselves.

Alley's hurt. Bad.

Mom and I found a safe space far enough from home. I managed to stop the bleeding for now. Afterwards, I had to step back. My hands wouldn't stop shaking. Mom took over. I have to get back to him. He needs me.

I hate you, Dad. Why did you have to be a general? Why did you have to be important?

I'm sorry, Dad. I don't hate you. It's not your fault. It's mine.

Alley always told me I'd need to protect myself someday. I should've listened. I promise I will. I just need him to be okay. He stayed because of me.

I don't think I can live with the idea of him dying for me.

Diary Entry # 32 – Infected

A.T. 269, Month 4, Day 07 (Tulan Standard Time)

I'm going to die.

This isn't just an update. This is the end. There's no way I can survive this. If I do, if I somehow live, I'm going to tell Alley the truth. I know he'll leave. Actually, I know he won't, but he should. I would.

Mom and I took Alley to a hospital. We carried him in, called over a nurse, and just left him.

Mom dropped him off, called Aunt Linda, and yanked me back to the velo before I could even kiss him goodbye. He nearly died to save me. He should get a kiss goodbye. Deal with it.

I fought Mom. Screamed in the middle of the hospital parking lot. She put me in a headlock and carried me out like I was a bag of grain. I can still feel her forearm crushing my windpipe.

When I tried to open the velo door to get out, she shocked me.

A neuro-static blast.

Not to communicate. To subdue. I never expected her to do that. I couldn't even try to defend myself. Strains of light and current overloaded every sense. For just a moment, I thought she was going to kill me, stop my heart. I know the Aquian heart has resistance to electric current, and apparently Mom not only knows that but has the proper voltage memorized.

It was excruciating.

When I came back to myself, finally coherent, we were miles away.

I screamed at her to turn around. We can't leave him. We can't leave Alley in a hospital three provinces away. She didn't say anything at first. She just found a hidden ridge and pulled over. Then she shut the engine off.

Then she said something I will **never** forget.

"You're a pathogen, Maria. He can't touch you without getting infected."

I don't think she meant it the way it sounded. She meant the Xaolin wouldn't be able to link him to us, not if we left now. The longer we stayed together, the more danger he was in. It didn't matter. I couldn't un-hear it.

"You're a pathogen." How could she call her own daughter that? For the first time in my life, I almost cursed my own mother to her face. The word was ready to go, in my mind and on its way to my mouth... then Mom broke down crying. Bawling. Wailing. The regal warrior was gone. The survivalist was gone. The mother was gone. She was just a vulnerable, terrified woman trying her best. The only thing I could do with my curse was turn it on myself.

She yelled that it wasn't easy. Asked if I thought it was easy to leave her son, her boy, behind to face whatever came. She reminded me she had been trying to help him and fighting for him years before we even met. Keeping him with us would have signed his death warrant. He's not on the target list.

I know she's right. I also know we left him alone.

Wounded.
Exposed.

And the worst part? She'd do it again.

We're in the mountains now. Somewhere quiet. Isolated. I don't even know where.

Mom's taken over my training. She's tougher than Alley. She doesn't slow down. Doesn't pull punches. Every time I think I've got a break, her staff catches my leg or shoulder in another three-hit combo.

She's surgical. Precise. Brutal. I want to rest, but I see Alley's face—ghost-white in my mind—and I ready up again. If I ever want to see the real thing, I need to be better. Not just smarter. Stronger.

We stopped at a supply post this afternoon. Mom asked for my smoke bomb recipe, then for a few other chemical tricks I've learned. Somehow, she stole some of my chemistry notes before I could burn them. She found some of the cocktails I'd sketched out—ones I swore I'd never make because of how dangerous they were. I told her about them, with reservations.

I told her to double-check my notes, not to trust my memory. I was tired. I wasn't confident. She ignored me. Said she didn't have time for my self-doubt. We got what we needed and made the chemical cocktails on a folded map and a metal tray.

We're sleeping in shifts under the stars now. Well, she's sleeping. I'm scared to sleep.

Every time I blink, I see that blade hovering over my bed, the one meant for me. I see Alley diving into it, throwing his body between me and death. In every nightmare I see between reprieves of starlight, he takes the blade and dies.

If there is a God—please.
Let me see him again. Alive.
Not just a memory.

Diary Entry # 33 – Ghost Signals

A.T. 269, Month 4, Day 10 (Tulan Standard Time)

I thought Mom was just running blind. We'd been traveling for days with no indication of where we were going. She never said a word, never even hinted at a destination. Just: drive. Wait. Move again.

When we finally stopped at the house, I realized something. This woman plans for everything.

It was some kind of safe house. I don't know if it's supplied by the army, the Kameonic government, or if it's just hers. It's fully stocked with food rations, weapons, med kits, comm gear, and scanning tech. Some of the equipment looks brand new, like it was released last month. One or two of these items aren't even supposed to be on the market yet.

Mom showed me where I'd be sleeping and left me there. Told me to "collect myself," whatever that's supposed to mean. The last thing I needed right now was to be alone. That's when the ghosts start haunting.

My specters were true to form.

I've seen Alley die so many times in my mind's eye, I hardly know if I'd believe it anymore, even if it really happened.

Mom found me sitting on the floor in the corner. I half expected her to lecture me again. Instead, she sat me down at the kitchen table with a pencil. "Draw something useful," was all she said before leaving again.

Vault Diary - Hypothesis Oblivion

What's useful? I started sketching out a comm sweeper. It just came to me. Comm sweepers are how this whole thing started. I would've stopped halfway through, but as long as my pencil was moving, the ghosts left me alone.

She saw the sketch. She didn't comment about safety protocols or dangers or what if you explode something. She just took me to the garage and said, "Good. We're on the same page. Build it. Anything you need that's not here, rig it up. Or I'll find it."

Then she added, "We need to know their next move. No communications. No signals. We're blind. Fix that."

She left again. This time I didn't have to wonder where. I saw her out the garage window. She walked into the woods, armed to the teeth: dual shield arm cannons, backup pistols, a sword at her hip, a blade on her boot. She looked more assassin than administrator. The ghosts returned the moment she vanished into the trees.

I did the only thing I could to get them away. I got to work. I'm rebuilding the comm scanner from scratch. Frequency cycling, broad-range signal interceptor, layered encryption trap. It's... weird how full circle this has gone. Mom used to ban me from experimenting. Now she's ordering me to build untested comms and theoretical explosives... in a garage. I guess that's survival.

I've made progress, but apparently not fast enough. Mom says we have two days, max. Then we move again. Too dangerous to stay in one place. We need to get off this planet.

I still can't sleep.

Every time I close my eyes, Alley's there. Not in a comforting way. Just… there. His voice. His laugh. That stupid smirk when he knows he's right.

Sometimes he says, "It's alright. Now you'll never get rid of me."

He laughs. Then the image warps. His voice distorts. His body twists. The memory turns into something more gruesome. I wake up shaking. I've apologized to his ghost a dozen times. He always forgives me. Every time I wake up, Mom is there watching, wide awake. She holds me close, without a word.

I asked Mom today why anyone would want to kill me. I think she tried to channel her inner Alley, crack a joke. It landed with the catastrophic weight of an asteroid. When she saw I couldn't laugh, she just… hugged me. Held me for a minute and whispered, "People are really after your dad. You're just leverage. We need to be strong and brave for him. He'll get us out. I'm following protocol."

So there's a plan. There's always a plan. I'm worried, but I'm even more exhausted. Maybe the haunting has finally caught up with me.

Maybe Mom dosed me. I wouldn't put it past her.

Diary Entry # 34 – I Did What I Was Told

A.T. 269, Month 4, Day 12 (Tulan Standard Time)

Mom wasn't wrong about how much time we had left. I finished the comm sweeper and convinced her to stay one more day so I could run a safe test. She agreed. I really wish she hadn't. Everything went fine. Perfect, actually. The sweeper worked better than expected. We were supposed to leave the next morning.

We never got the chance. At least, not the way I expected.

I woke up yesterday to a glowing symbol next to my bed. Mom had put a run signal on the wall: two infinities, one vertical, one horizontal, arrow pointed away. How she activated it, I don't know. She must've seen something on patrol.

I can't believe I'm writing this—I actually did what I was told.

I grabbed what I could:

> My scanning kit
> My rations
> My double-sticks
> A shield arm cannon
> This diary and a pen

Why did I grab you? Can't give our pursuers any information. Yeah, let's go with that.

The velo was gone, so I ran. I ran for hours. I don't even know who I was running from. I swear I heard something explode in the distance after twenty minutes. I keep telling myself that was a mining blast. It can't be the alternative.

I don't know how many trees blurred past me. I stuck to the deep forest, staying out of sight of roads and paths, until I got lost. I didn't have time to panic. I just found a ridgeline, stayed with it, and prayed I wasn't circling.

I stopped only when my heart was three beats from detonation—barely able to stand, let alone breathe. I ate. Threw up. Ate again. Threw up again. At some point I just gave up. "Fine. The worms can win."

I didn't even know where I was. It took me half the day to find a strong enough signal to get a rough location. I'm about two weeks' journey, on foot, from the Rain Province. Going home… given everything… is probably not an option.

It's getting dark now. I found a cave to hide in. It's more like a coal mine, really. Abandoned. Quiet. Cold. Can't light a fire. My chemical tests show there are odorless gases in the air. One wrong spark and I die before the next sentence.

I can't sleep. I'm trying, but the ghosts are back with a vengeance. I'm scared. Not anxious. Not nervous. Terrified.

How could Mom leave me like this? Is this my life now? Is this it?

Am I going to die out here in a cave like some old hermit maid, eating trout and squirrel pellets, writing equations in the dirt?

Vault Diary - Hypothesis Oblivion

Will the Xaolin find me?

Honestly, maybe I deserve it. I was the one who brought them here, wasn't I? I mean, who'd care? Who's left?

Alley… we left him like debris on a battlefield. I don't know if he lived. I don't know if he's still out there, waiting for us, or if that last dive was the last thing he ever did.

Mom sent the signal. That's all I know. She could be dead too. Blast debris in the wind.

Dad? He can't be gone. He's not allowed to die. I have to say, and I cannot believe I'm writing this, but I want my daddy.

I just want to curl into his arms and sleep. Not think. Not plan. Not fight.

Just sleep. Just peace.

I don't want this life.

Diary Entry # 35 – Extraction

A.T. 269, Month 4, Day 25 (Galactic Standard Time)

I know I have a tendency to be too hard on myself. I wasn't exactly born into a warzone, but I knew my parents were both war adjacent. I should've prepared myself. I'm also sleep deprived.

I didn't know what else to do yesterday morning. I'd been hiding in those mines for almost two weeks. I thought someone would come. No such luck, and I was out of rations. I reached the support town outside the mines just after first light. If I'd had to spend one more hour down there, I would've gone insane. The support town had more specters than the safe house. There was nothing there: no answers, no guidance. Just wind, dirt, and a hundred wrong ideas.

I had no plan. Then I saw a transport. The driver had stopped in town for supplies and let it slip he was heading to Liviton. I walked away without a word, climbed into the cargo bay, and hid between barrels of corn and grain. No one checked. I don't even know how long the trip was. Two days, maybe more. The driver never even looked back.

I didn't go home. I wasn't that stupid. What I did was worse.

I went to Alley's house. He wasn't there. Neither were Aunt Linda or Uncle Quince. I walked right in through the unlocked door. In retrospect, I lied. I was that stupid. How did I not know, with the door open, that there was a problem?

Not thirty seconds later, I heard the door slam shut. I hit the lights and saw them: five Xaolin assassins, the gleam in their eyes. Nearly a week of nightmares now, that image on repeat. I already knew their objective. Take me dead or alive. The way they gripped their daggers, they clearly preferred the former.

I ran to the back room and managed to lock the doors. For a minute, it worked. They tried their shoulders against the frame before realizing their weapons would serve them better. That gave me just enough time to climb to the second floor. When they broke in, I tossed a smoke bomb. It burst right in front of them.

What happened next, I've been trying to sort out ever since. I turned on my shield arm cannon. I had a clear shot. The smoke had them stumbling and coughing. They'd never get away in time. I had one lined up. My weapon was aimed, powered, ready.

I couldn't fire.

Not at a person. Not even to save myself. Something in me just stopped. What is wrong with me? These people are trying to kill me. They would kill my mother if they haven't already. They would kill my best friend, my father, everyone I care about. Why couldn't I fire? It haunts me now, but at the time I just accepted it. I had to make a plan that didn't involve death on either side. I had to get away.

I ran to the attic. The stairs behind me were still intact, and they were coming. I did the only thing I could. I turned and fired, not at them but at the staircase. The whole thing exploded in a burst of shrapnel and heat.

The blast caught me.

I flew backward into a wall. Hit it hard. Everything blurred. I was dizzy, hurt, disoriented, breathing smoke and adrenaline.

And then he showed up.

Lieutenant Colonel Vaughn. My dad's friend.

He entered the house like he was cutting through shadows—precise, controlled, not a motion wasted. He neutralized all five of them like they were made of air. By the time he made it to the attic, I thought I was hallucinating.

He stepped onto the broken stool at the base of the blown-out staircase and launched himself into the attic like a cat. I just stared, no idea if I was seeing straight.

Then he said my full name. Gave his full rank, serial number, procedure, purpose.

Okay, maybe not a cat. More like a lion. A force of nature. Aggression and presence in perfect balance. Or maybe that's just my concussed brain making metaphors. But I noticed. I couldn't not.

He knew where to find me. Said he figured I'd go to Alley's place because that's what he would've done when he was my age.

"He's your safest anchor," he said. "Even when he's not there."

Then his voice softened. His whole body language shifted. From soldier to caretaker in an instant.

He wrapped me in a thermal cloak and started treating my shoulder and back. Said the impact trauma wasn't serious, but I'd feel it for a few days. His hands were gentle. His voice even more so. Fine, I'll admit it. I let myself melt for a moment in his arms. Take from that what you will, diary.

He handed me something: Dad's rank insignia. Said he was ordered to give it to me when I was safe. I almost cried. He carried me out of the house. Outside, army patrols swept every street—perimeter sealed tight.

And then I saw him.

Alley.

He was waiting at the perimeter. And right behind him, Mom.

She's here. Physically here. With me. With all of us. Uncle Quince brought his ship around as the army turned the residence into a landing port. We didn't go back to the Rain Province. We left it behind. I'm staying with Alley now, aboard their ship with Aunt Linda, Uncle Quince, and Mom.

We were in orbit for an hour, an entire armada surrounding us. The safest I've felt since this whole thing began. Dad called. Told Mom to leave the investigation to him. She scoffed and stormed out. Telling an Inquisitor not to inquire has to be the worst insult. This is going to be a long trip. He didn't say much to me, just apologized and said he was proud. For what? Surviving? I'm getting default pride now? At least I know he's okay.

The armada took us as far as the edge of the Peiyai Sector and ordered us to stay mobile. So we are. Constantly moving. Still running. Just in space now. Great. I hate space travel.

I found Mom in a guest room Aunt Linda was setting up for us. Mom sat me down to recheck my shoulder. Vaughn had already handled the worst of it: burns, bruises, strain. I really wanted her to leave it, but she insisted. Checked everything again. Quiet. Focused. No words. For a second, I thought maybe this was it, just treatment, just care. I knew something was wrong when she kept lingering and staring at Aunt Linda until she got the hint and left.

What followed was the longest thirty seconds of my life. It was like she didn't know what to say but had to say something. Every time I tried to get up, she pressed on my bad shoulder until I gave up. So I waited.

"Why didn't you shoot?" I opened my mouth and froze. How could she ask me that? There was no one to defend. No one, just me. I must have waited too long to answer.

"The assassin. Why didn't you shoot?"

"I couldn't. I couldn't do it."

She didn't blink.

"Next time, you will." I can't place what I saw in her eyes when she said it. A rare mix of authority and desperation. Cold. Unshakable. Not a suggestion. More like a threat. Still, within it was the slightest hint of understanding.

"I can't," I whispered. She grabbed me again by my injured shoulder and pulled me close until our eyes locked.

"They weren't coming to scare you, Maria. They were coming to kill you."

"I know." The glare that started the conversation shifted into something more inquisitive, horrified, and almost a little proud. She didn't just look into my eyes; she searched them, as if the answer to erase my selfish morality was buried inside.

"The moment you know that, you fire. You don't wait for permission. You end the threat." Then she turned away and left, like it was settled. It wasn't.

That stuck with me.

It still does. I nodded like I understood. I don't. Not yet. Maybe I never will. Honestly, I don't want to, because even now, with everything we've seen, I still can't do it.

Funny to think this all started with some unrecognizable static. The signals are clear now, decoded and real. That doesn't mean I understand them.

Story 006: Exile

The hardest times in my life weren't when people were trying to kill me. I had plenty of that... strangely, it wasn't so bad. The objective was usually pretty clear: stay alive, protect what matters. The time in between... that was the real war zone. The people who loved me... those were the hardest to fight. As a child, I couldn't escape my mother, deny my father, defy my aunt, or abandon my best friend. I had to live in their reality. They were my anchors. My greatest demon was myself, and in the world of self-destruction, my demon's ultimate weapon was my anchors.

Diary Entry # 36 – Echoes in Orbit

A.T. 269, Month 4, Day 40 (Galactic Standard Time)

I think I'm starting to lose my mind.
Which is a shame, really… my mind was always my favorite part of me.

We've been chasing comets for a week now. We've got maybe three more weeks of materials before we run out, assuming nothing goes wrong. I think I've slept a total of twenty hours the entire time. Half sedated. Half mid-sprint, running for my life in dreams that never let me go.

Every time I close my eyes, I wake up choking on smoke or staring down a shield arm cannon, feeling that blade at my neck. Every night I watch someone I love, Mom, Dad, Alley, sometimes me, get struck down. The faces change. Each death is more gruesome. I'm always there. Frozen. Watching. Every night… and space doesn't really have days.

I wake up shaking. Crying. Screaming. I spend more time hysterical than logical now. I don't think living off-planet is helping. Mom is trying to keep us on Tulan Standard Time. Aunt Linda, Uncle Quince, and Alley have their own way of working out here, and it's not compatible.

Mom's getting restless too. She's used to being Queen of the Castle. Out here, she's a passenger. A peasant. She and Aunt Linda fight constantly, more than I've ever seen. Aunt Linda blames her for all this. It doesn't help. I know… I tried blaming Dad.

The people hunting us? They want us just as dead.

Alley's trying. He really is. When he's not training or running piloting drills, he checks in on me, makes jokes, brings me things from the mess like a starship waiter with no tips. He's fraying too. He's not used to dealing with my mom this much. The constant bickering. The inevitable blow-up. The half-hearted apology just to keep the peace till the next landmine.

If we don't get off this ship soon, someone's going to mutiny. They'll find the vessel adrift, all of us dead, just frozen mid-throttle, hands around each other's throats. If the Xaolin want us dead, this isn't a bad contingency plan for them.

I spend most of the day in the engine room now. It's the only place that makes sense. Aunt Linda comes down sometimes to check on me, tries to get me to eat. I said no to her food yesterday.

I said no to Aunt Linda's cooking. I must be crazy. She makes army rations taste like gourmet meals.

Uncle Quince asked if he could hire me. Said the engines have never run this well. I think he's just trying to keep me busy, but I don't care. I know I said I was done with science, but this isn't an invention. It's maintenance. And it's... *soothing.*

It's like therapy.

Mom's been pacing. Watching the stars too much. The Xaolin haven't hit us again yet, but they're subcontracting now, outsourcing our deaths like it's some kind of open market.

The bigger this gets, the harder it'll be to stop.

The army hasn't told us anything. Not a word. Just silence and stars and more silence.

Somebody has to come up with a plan before the void swallows us whole.

Diary Entry # 37 – When She Left Me

A.T. 269, Month 4, Day 43 (Galactic Standard Time)

I hit my mom today. More than once. Too many times. She deserved it.

I guess I should start at the beginning.

I went to the cockpit just to see where we were headed, right after breakfast. (Yes, I actually ate. For once.) It was the first night I'd slept through since this all started. I guess the ghosts decided to take the night off, or my brain was too exhausted after a week of sleepless nights for hallucinations.

I was about to step inside when I heard voices. Mom and Aunt Linda. They didn't see me yet.

Mom said she had a lead. A real one. On who hired the Xaolin. She asked Aunt Linda to chart a course for Voltaire III. As much as I was ready to get off the ship, Voltaire III was the last place I wanted to do it. Might as well set down at Xaolin headquarters and bring a spare knife in a gift box.

Aunt Linda pushed back, said she didn't like it. Mom wasn't having it. She said it was to bring this to an end. I think she just couldn't take another day living with Aunt Linda. I cannot understand how the closest women I have ever known could hate each other so much. I know they would die for each other.

When Mom held her ground, Aunt Linda insisted I should stay with her. "She's barely holding together," she told Mom. "Being with Alley right now might actually help her."

Mom answered, "Then keep your kid on a leash." I heard something scratch, something move, loud, sudden. I imagined Aunt Linda lunging for her throat, but probably not.

"Your daughter's just as much a troublemaker as my son." That would've hurt more if I wasn't still trying to process Mom abandoning me.

I don't know what gave me away. The crying… it was probably the crying. The door flung open, and I fell through.

I asked if it was true the moment I was settled.

She tried to turn it on me, scolded me for eavesdropping, and tried to send me away. I didn't move. I asked again if she was really leaving.

She said yes.

I asked to go with her. She said no.

I asked again. No.

I begged. No.

I asked her how she could do this, how she could abandon me now, after everything.

"I'm protecting you, Maria. This is for your own good."

Leaving me in the middle of nowhere to run around Voltaire III, is for me? Right.

She said where she's going is dangerous. Too dangerous for me.

That's when I lost it. I screamed. Pleaded.

And then I hit her. I don't even know how many times. She didn't raise her hand. Didn't yell. For a while, she just let me do it, even as I struck her harder and harder.

She grabbed my wrists when my hits turned into clumsy punches. She pulled me into a bear hug and held me still, the kind of hold I'd expect from Dad if I lost it. She didn't let go.

I screamed when Aunt Linda said, "Quince, set course for Voltaire III."

Curse those tuned engines. He had the ship going full speed, and we were there within two hours. I swear, Mom held me almost the entire time. Aunt Linda packed for her.

When the ship touched down and she had to get off, I put her in a bear hug. Interlocked my fingers. Alley and Uncle Quince had to pull me off her.

"I'm sorry, Maria." Those are the last words my mother said to me.

I'm in the cockpit now. Alone. Alley got my diary, and I hoped that writing would give me clarity. Not happening. I don't even recognize myself.

Vault Diary - Hypothesis Oblivion

I'm sitting here in this dark room, staring at the controls. Every part of me wants to turn the ship around. To go after her. To fix this. To scream until she comes back.

I can't.

I don't know what to do. How could she leave me? Now of all times?

Mom… you traitor.

Please tell me I will see you again.

Diary Entry # 38 – What I've Made

A.T. 269, Month 4, Day 49 (Galactic Standard Time)

It's been two days since Mom left.

(Yes, I'm still using Tulan Standard Time. Sue me. I am on Mom's side. That, and there is no way I'm writing a new entry every 11 hours.)

I miss her more than I thought I would.

Actually, it's not even that I miss her. I'm worried.

She didn't give me much to go on. No plan. No timeline. No explanation. The last time I saw her, while I was clinging to her like a toddler, she was armed to the teeth. I think the only reason she didn't throw me off was because she was afraid she might accidentally kill me.

Her energy shield clipped me during the struggle. I still have a cut across my cheek from Mom's armor.

I never knew how hardcore she is. If we weren't running for our lives, I might even think she was cool. If I didn't hate her right now, she'd be my hero.

I've been living in the engine room. I know more about spaceship mechanics now than I think anyone without a pilot's license should. Honestly, I think I could miniaturize most of the tech. The bulky size does a number on energy efficiency. Boost the plasma injection ratio, double the shield output with a tighter energy transfer system... even on this ship. I'm sketching out a nine-point cycle. Still needs testing.

Vault Diary - Hypothesis Oblivion

I told Alley and Uncle Quince about it. Uncle Quince stared at me.

Alley asked, "When do we start construction?" First time I've laughed in two weeks. This is a dream sketch. Building this would cost a fortune. Uncle Quince sent Alley to help Aunt Linda in the cockpit.

Then he sat down with me, just us, in the engine room. He asked why I was down here, rebuilding his engines, if I'd given up science. Seriously, who did Alley not tell? I told him it was just repairs. I think I needed to believe that. He wasn't convinced. Didn't say a word. Just gave me that cynical look. It was enough.

I cracked. Told him the truth.

That I start inventing, then stop. Then start again. Then stop. That every invention I've made has hurt something. The dark space collector? Almost killed me. It got Dr. Childs killed too, the first person to believe in me despite my age.

The harvester upgrade? Blew out a quarter of our crops. My fertilizer? Destroyed the rest of the harvest and killed a man. I should stick to baking cakes.

I was shaking. Crying. I said I was cursed.

He held me. Didn't argue, just held me. I don't know how he knew what I needed, but it had to be the first free breath I'd taken in weeks.

When I was out of tears, he dried my eyes like he was my father. I didn't stop him. Maybe I didn't want to. I can see where Alley gets it now. He smiled, then lifted my head to meet his eyes.

"You are a blessing, not a curse." He let me hear him and not believe him. It was like he knew he had to get that out of the way. Then he started going through my list with new eyes.

The collector saved lives. It forced the Xaolin to change tactics. The harvester revolutionized fuel efficiency. Farmers across Tula would thank me. The fire outed a fraudulent distributor before their poisons made it to dinner tables.

"Jenkave's death was a tragedy," he said. "But it was an accident. And you tried to stop it. So did Alley, almost at the cost of his life. If we'd known how desperate he was, we would've helped him."

Then he said something I haven't stopped hearing since:

"You haven't made things worse, Maria. You gave us a warning. Your frequency scanner is the only reason any of us are alive. You gave us a chance. You gave us life. You've just been too myopic to see it."

I wish I didn't see through it—that attempt to lift the guilt off me. "The Xaolin wouldn't be after you if it wasn't for us."

"True." I didn't expect him to own that. I expected a deflection. He just hugged me again.

"If you think we'd let you face them alone, you're crazy. You're one of us."

He got up to leave. "Design your shield. When you're ready, I'll fund it. Whatever it takes, as long as I get to use it first." We shared a laugh, weak though it was.

Just before he walked out, he added, "Don't stop creating, Maria. You have a gift. Hiding it is a slap in God's face." Then he was gone.

I don't know what to say. Or think. Or do.

Right now, I don't care about God. I just want to live long enough to make it back to school for Physics II.

Hopefully, not as an orphan.

Diary Entry # 39 – Ten Minutes

A.T. 269, Month 4, Day 52 (Galactic Standard Time)

I swear the Xaolin must've overheard my conversation with Uncle Quince, like they were trying to prove him right. I picked up their signal on my scanner. They were coming.

We had ten minutes. It was enough.

Uncle Quince had us all in the cockpit, and strapped in. I've never seen someone move like that. He is one of the most impressive pilots I have ever seen. Three Xaolin fighters came after us. He took out all three, clean and precise.

I see what Mom meant when she told me to take the shot. He didn't shoot to disarm or disable. Every shot went straight for the engines. No hesitation. No mercy. No second chances. I don't know why I'm thrown by the fact that they're dead.

The alternative was us.

He flew us into a cavernous moon two sectors away. We're hiding there now.

Somehow, I'm supposed to sleep after that.

Uncle Quince shut down all non-emergency power. Said the ship's almost undetectable now. Anything we need, we have to power manually.

Vault Diary - Hypothesis Oblivion

He's taking first watch over the sensors. Told me to sleep in the engine room so I can adjust power if needed. Like I wasn't sleeping there already.

Alley's in here with me. He's training again, for the next tournament.

I don't get him sometimes. We might not live to next week, and he's preparing for something two years from now. He asked me if I was up for a spar. Insisted it would be a good stress reliever. I called nonsense, but I agreed, mostly to make him happy.

It did. It made him happy.

I'll admit, hitting him was more cathartic than I'll ever confess to his face. It made me feel almost normal for two minutes. I think he knew. He let me land three more hits than he should have. He's faster than that.

The nightmares are getting worse. I don't usually remember them. The ability to forget nightmares is the one mercy God gave Aquians.

I write them down sometimes just to make sure they're not trying to tell me something. Sometimes they are. By day's end, I don't remember what happened, just how they feel. I wake up shaking, nauseated, ready to scream. Sometimes I don't sleep at all. Now, even that's not helping.

The nightmares come when I'm awake.

I flinch at phantom sounds. Cringe when I open a door. I jumped at a coolant hiss earlier and nearly slammed my head on the reactor wall. I had to stop sparring with Alley. I choked him. Full-on. Not a choke hold, not a lock—my hand around his neck, trying to squeeze the life out of him.

For a split second, I thought he was trying to kill me.

He had to *throw* me off. He almost broke my wrist breaking my grip. Even then, I'm not sure I stopped right away.

He just said, "That's enough for today."

Didn't blame me.
Didn't flinch.
Just held me. Let me fall apart. Ignored every apology.

If we ever get out of this…

I'll need therapy until I'm thirty.

Vault Diary - Hypothesis Oblivion

Diary Entry # 40 – A Breath

A.T. 269, Month 4, Day 55 (Galactic Standard Time)

Short entry today. Not much happened. We stayed low. I think the Xaolin have finally given up.

They're heading away. I saw it on the scanner.

We're moving in the morning.

I had the first nightmare that I fully remember.

I was in the mine, back on Tula. This time, I wasn't alone. Alley was there. So were Mom and Dad. Then they left. One at a time. Quiet. No explanation. Just gone.

I waited. Until I couldn't. When I finally followed, there they were—the assassins. All of them. Holding the same blade, that curved sickle the first one used. The one who stood over my bed that night, back in the Rain Province. I still see that blade when I close my eyes. Feel his hand pressing, the sharp cold metal edge on my neck.

Every time I blink, I can't breathe.

Alley, if you ever read this, you are never allowed to doubt yourself in my presence again. You nearly threw your life away just for the chance to save mine, and you did. That means you don't get to apologize. Ever. I won't allow it.

In the dream, I ran back into the mine. Tried to throw a smoke bomb. It exploded an instant later. It exploded. The mine collapsed. I was buried alive. Couldn't move. Couldn't scream. Just watched the beams above me buckle, then fall. Felt the crush.

I woke up soaked, shaking, sobbing, choking. Couldn't run. Couldn't be. Alley was already there. He didn't say anything, just sent Aunt Linda and Uncle Quince away and held me until I remembered how to breathe. It felt like two years. It was probably two hours.

Aunt Linda got us to eat. Then she pulled out a board game. Simple. Quiet. Old. I'd never seen anything like it. We played. They laughed. Told stories. Teased each other. They were so at ease, like this was their ritual.

I blended in somehow. It helped. Is this what normal looks like? Maybe that's why it hits so hard. I never considered how dysfunctional my family actually is. Not ready to unpack that yet.

Not tonight.

Vault Diary - Hypothesis Oblivion

Diary Entry # 41 – Something's Wrong

A.T. 269, Month 4, Day 58 (Galactic Standard Time)

Dad finally called. He said the words I didn't know I'd been waiting to hear: "They found the person who put the hit on us."

He's being held at Centrum. Dad wants us to go there immediately. I should feel relieved. I should feel safe. All I feel is wrong. Something about this doesn't make sense. Not the timing. Not the tone. Not the silence underneath it.

Aunt Linda and Uncle Quince are ecstatic. They already set a course for Kameon Central. We'll be there in a few days. Alley's already making a checklist like this is just another mission.

Me?

I spent most of the evening in the engine room. Not to work. Not to tweak or build or repair. Just to be alone.

I keep asking myself, where is Mom? Maybe this means there was a breakthrough in her investigation. Maybe that's how they found the client. Maybe she's okay. So why didn't Dad say so? Why didn't he mention her? Maybe he doesn't know she left. Then why didn't he ask about her?

Alright. Two trains. Let's pick one before they both derail.

Train One: If he's in touch, why not let me know how she is? Not a single word. Not even a vague "she's fine." If she found the people after us, he'd lead with that. If there's one thing my dad does, it's brag about Mom.

Train Two: If he's not in touch with her, the first thing he would want would be to see her. Even if he figured she's fine, he would want verification. When the hit was put out on us, he always needed to see her before he would begin talking to us.

Something is off. I'll update you, diary.

Diary Update:

I asked Uncle Quince to call him back. Told him I had a bad feeling. He didn't even argue. Said we had to conserve power, but he made the call. That's when everything fell apart.

Dad didn't know we were en route. He never called us. The message we got didn't come from him. I saw him. I saw someone who looked like him. He kept himself mostly off screen, supposedly working interrogation. If the Xaolin are resorting to these tactics, they must be getting desperate.

When we told him Mom was out there, that we hadn't heard from her in nine days (Galactic Time), he lost it. He ended the call mid-sentence, practically growling.

"That woman…" That's all I heard.

Something is very, very wrong.

I asked what we should do next. We found cover in a dark nebula and shut everything down. So far, no sign we're being followed. We're running low on supplies, and now

Centrum's the nearest port. If this was a trap, they'll be waiting. If it wasn't, we're about to miss our only chance at answers.

Aunt Linda feels it's too dangerous to go to Centrum. Uncle Quince thinks flying blindly back might be just as risky as pushing forward. He said the words we've all been avoiding:

"If the Xaolin could smuggle a call to us, we can't rely on anything we hear from command. We might have to go rogue."

Honestly, I think we already are.

I don't know what comes next. I just hope it brings answers. Right now, all I've got is this feeling.

My reprieve is coming to a sudden end.

None of this is over. The warning is ringing in my ears. I'm waking now to echoes of dread. My nightmares are quiet lately. That's worse. I don't trust silence.

Not anymore.

Diary Entry # 42 – Votes and Weak Spots

A.T. 269, Month 4, Day 61 (Galactic Standard Time)

Aunt Linda made the deciding vote. She said she wouldn't leave her sister out there.

We're going to find Mom. Mom told Aunt Linda she had a contact on Voltaire III, a trader in information. She says he knows a little bit about everything. A broker. Figures we should start there. Alley asked why we couldn't just reach out to someone named Strand. Apparently, he's the guy you talk to when things go sideways.

Aunt Linda agreed but said he's on Centrum, the last place we want to be right now. Uncle Quince disagreed. Said Strand was more reliable. Safer. More military-adjacent. Less likely to burn us. Thought we should risk going to Centrum. Alley sided with his dad.

They gave me two votes, since it's my mom. Final count: three to two, we're going to Voltaire III.

I've never felt quite so seen. I guess seeing people runs in their family. I was half afraid they would guilt me over my choice, especially after Aunt Linda sided with me. All that was said came from Uncle Quince to Alley:

"You know what to do."

Apparently, in the Jabez household, that means suit up for war.

The ship was alive today. Busy. Focused. Preparing.

Vault Diary - Hypothesis Oblivion

I spent most of the day packing rations, recalibrating the engine flow controls, and helping Alley prep for recon. Apparently, he and Uncle Quince insist on going over the landing plan twice. Minimum. Uncle Quince doesn't like where we're going. That much is very clear.

The only thing he knows about Voltaire III is a place called the Smugglers' Outpost. That's where we'll go. It's a kind of neutral zone, not controlled by any of the intergalactic powers. The more he described the place, the more I knew I wasn't ready to go there.

According to him, it's the kind of place where anything goes, and no one will come to save you if things go wrong. I'd say how is that different from here and now, but I still have this family. Apparently, things can still get worse. Of course they can.

We're on our own.

Alley spent the rest of the day training with me. It was different this time — anatomy. Weak points. He walked me through where to strike and how, and I had to demonstrate each one. Which meant he had to take blows on each one until I got it right.

I felt bad. I really had to hit him. He only hit me when I hesitated. My hands were shaking after each strike. I hated learning this way. We couldn't move on to the next weak point until I subdued him.

He didn't complain. Winced a few times. Said if we got into a fight, he needed to know I knew how and where to strike. He needed me to be reliable.

I will be.
I promise.
I hope.

He stumbled into dinner like he'd just finished a prize match. Uncle Quince asked if I was "combat ready," and Alley gave a full assessment—very clinical, all business. Did an impression of me. Terrible. I elbowed his ribs.

He groaned. "That's better," he said.

I laughed. Then we both did.

I've been dreading sleep since the first night on this ship. Tonight, not so much. I think tonight I'll actually rest.

We're going to find Mom. I don't know if everything will be okay, but at least we're not running anymore.

We're fighting back. That's better.

Story 007: The Smuggler's Outpost

If my childhood ended when the Xaolin came home, Voltaire III is where I grew up. Until then, I was a child trying to survive in an adult world. That wasteland gave me a choice: die an idealist or live with the scraps of morality I could scavenge. The questions children don't think to ask often have the most unpalatable answers.

This was my first real adventure. I've had many since, more than I care to remember. People who romanticize adventure have never bled through one. Voltaire wasn't survival training or tactical strategy; it was a plunge into a world that didn't care whether I escaped or disappeared inside.

Vault Diary - Hypothesis Oblivion

Diary Entry # 43 – The Outpost

A.T. 269, Month 4, Day 13 (Voltaire Standard Time)

We landed just outside the Smugglers' Outpost. My stomach knotted before the ramp even lowered. The environment didn't help. Shifting from artificial to natural gravity wasn't dramatic, just a 2% differential, but I felt it in every step, like a permanent weight or wind, an invisible thick fog. Even a short stroll left me winded. How were we supposed to save Mom in this?

I thought I'd be the only one on edge. I was wrong. I've never seen Uncle Quince so tense.

Turns out this place is where Aunt Linda did her shipping before they met. From the way he talks, not all of it was strictly legal. Before we disembarked, he called a family meeting.

Two rules:

1. I'm Alley's responsibility, just as Aunt Linda is Quince's. Apparently that's code for *"no hero moves, no questions."* Sure.

2. Stay out of sight. Say nothing. (Apparently that rule is just for Alley and me.)

Alley moved like he owned the place. He led me up a fire escape, across a rooftop, through a back door, and into ductwork. His mom used to run them through back channels. Alley's done this before. "Strand's different," he told me. "Uncle Strand treats us like family. He even keeps a room for us in case we ever stop by."

We caught up to Aunt Linda's contact, and I get now why Uncle Quince hates this place.

The guy is unsettling. All cryptic grins and shadowy metaphors. He treated Uncle Quince like an afterthought and wouldn't give a straight answer to anything. Info about Mom would cost. Everything does out here. Quince was ready for that. Paid the contact on the spot, no hesitation.

The contact told us to come back tomorrow. Said he had to *"check his sources."*

As we walked out, Uncle Quince gave his hand signal, flicked two fingers over his head. All clear.

The moment we were back on the ship, his first words were, "We're leaving. He's got nothing." I didn't understand. Aunt Linda insisted we'd already paid, so we might as well wait and see what he finds. Uncle Quince was certain the guy wasn't going to help. "He's playing us," he said. "I paid more so we could walk away, not for what he's selling. That guy sees a mark, not a client."

In the end, he only stayed because I asked him to. He reminded us we'd all agreed. Before turning in, he told Alley, "If things go south, take her and run. You know what to do. Your mom taught you well." I don't know what that meant. I mean, I hope I don't know what that meant. I'm starting to wonder if I'll ever see normal again. I definitely know there are some stories my "aunt" and "uncle" haven't told me.

I'm supposed to sleep now. How?

Uncle Quince is sitting up, eyes wide, arm cannon pointed at the landing ramp.

Aunt Linda suggested we sleep in orbit. Quince shut that down. She's drifting at the scan station.

Alley's feeding off his dad's energy. He's sleeping on the floor, his body a physical doorstop.

I can't believe I almost miss the ghosts. At least those threats belonged to a past I'd already survived. This feels worse. I just want my life back.

Diary Entry # 44 – The Price of a Lead

A.T. 269, Month 4, Day 14 (Voltaire Standard Time)

We finally made some progress today, or so I thought. You'd think Uncle Quince would feel better, at least a little. Instead, he's been in the ship's supply room all evening, going over his weapons again and again like he's waiting for a war to break out.

We went back to the meeting spot, just like the trader told us. Alley and I headed straight for our hiding place in the attic. This time, the contact had the place cleared. No guards. Just him. He said it was better to speak in private. At first, I didn't understand why, until he smiled directly at me. I froze. Didn't make a sound. He couldn't see me, could he? It was like he was in my head. He even winked the moment I asked the question in my mind. I thought I was hidden. Somehow, he knew.

"Good day, Mistress Maze... or is it Mistress Roamai? You still carry your father's name, don't you?" The trader raised his voice and his arm cannon, pointing it straight at Aunt Linda. "I know you've got the kids watching. Go on, let's put all our cards on the table."

Uncle Quince stepped in front of the barrel, grabbed it, and pressed it to his chest.

"Go," Quince ordered. He pointed toward the door, and Aunt Linda ran for it without hesitation.

"Bring Maria down here. No harm will befall the heiress, I assure you."

How was this worse than having the blade at my neck? What was I supposed to do? I turned to Alley. I was his responsibility, right? He shifted position and told me to stay put. I followed orders.

The trader smirked, insisting he didn't want to do it this way. "I don't make deals with prying eyes watching. You can understand that."

Uncle Quince asked the trader to lower his weapon. He did so without hesitation. Uncle Quince gave the signal for me to come down, a single flick of his hand toward me with two fingers. I ran down there. It took at least twenty turns to get down; it felt like one long tunnel with a firing squad at the end.

When I arrived, the trader made his offer. He said he had a source who knew where Mom was. The person holding her had promised her to the Xaolin. The price on Mom's head was three million credits. If we could offer five, they were willing to let her go. "The Maze family fortune should more than cover that," he said.

Uncle Quince immediately refused. No deal. Not even a pause. I couldn't stay quiet. I asked the question we were all thinking: "How do we know you're telling the truth?"

The contact didn't answer directly. He only said to meet him again tomorrow, that he would arrange the exchange.

"Fine." Uncle Quince stood and motioned for us to leave, Aunt Linda still half in shock. We were nearly out the door when the trader added, "Next time, don't leave anyone in the rafters."

When I looked back, I saw Uncle Quince standing with his arms folded. I could feel the trader's glare from behind him as he raised his arm cannon toward the attic. Was Alley still hiding there?

"We're leaving," Quince said, projecting his voice. "Let him go." I heard some movement, too far to the left to be where the cannon was pointed. What did that mean? Who was letting who go?

When Uncle Quince finally turned back to me, the look on his face, full of fury and disgust, told me everything. I knew he was done. He has barely said a word to me since.

We spent the rest of the day chasing shadows. Aunt Linda dragged us through alley after alley, calling in every old contact she could. Everyone said the same thing: he's legit. He used to be reliable. That "used to be" keeps bothering me.

When we got back to the ship, we found it ransacked.
Nothing stolen.
Everything searched.

Uncle Quince scolded me. "Next time, keep your mouth shut."

"Quince!" That was the beginning and end of their argument. He pulled Aunt Linda aside and told her to keep an eye on the kids, then locked himself in the weapons room. He hasn't come out since. She went in after him about an hour later.

When she came out, something had changed. She didn't say anything. She just moved through the ship like she finally remembered what it felt like to breathe.

Aunt Linda seems steadier now, calmer, more hopeful. I don't know what they said or did, but it worked. I wish I could find that kind of peace, even for an hour.

I don't know what I've gotten us into. All I wanted was to find my mom. Now... I don't even know if this guy really knows anything.

What if Quince is right? What if I just got us locked in a deathmatch with a conman?

Where does that leave us? How do we escape it?

Diary Entry # 45 – Smoke and Mirrors

A.T. 269, Month 4, Day 15 (Voltaire Standard Time)

I should've known. Mom always said the most dangerous moment is right after you start to feel safe. That's when you stop paying attention. That's when the worst things happen.

We met our source at the agreed location. He wasn't alone. One guy with him. Tall. Muscled. Dead-eyed. Uncle Quince walked in unarmed.

They checked him.
They checked me.
They asked for the money. Quince said no. No proof, no payment.
They asked again. Same response.

Then the trap sprung. Men came from everywhere. Shadows from the walls, the corners, the rooftops. They took me first, then Uncle Quince. He didn't look surprised. "Do as told," he whispered, quiet but deadly serious.

They searched the building from top to bottom. Couldn't find Aunt Linda or Alley. Someone asked for the money again. Not from Quince. From me.

They knew I had the Maze family fortune access codes. They weren't wrong. I did. But I only knew one thing I was supposed to do. "Next time, keep your mouth shut." Uncle Quince's warning echoed in my ear as loud as the men holding us.

Convinced I needed persuading, they slammed Uncle Quince to the ground and asked again. I hesitated.

"Do as told," Uncle Quince repeated. I stayed quiet until they said they would kill him. Find his family. Kill them too. I gave them the code. Actually, first I begged them... begged... to let Uncle Quince go. I promised I'd give them everything if they just let him walk.

Uncle Quince protested. They agreed. They let him go.

I can't even remember why I asked. Maybe I thought if I was going to die, at least Alley wouldn't lose us both. Maybe I wasn't thinking at all.

Through most of it, all I remember is the arm cannon barrel drilling into my back. How cold it felt through my shirt. How much pressure they used to press it into the same spot, over and over, until I could barely stand straight.

They took me to a bank and promised they'd kill me if the code didn't work. It did.

When they tried to pull five million credits, it only let them take fifty thousand. Turns out my access code only allows small withdrawals.

Must've been one of Mom's limits... a quiet kill switch. I didn't know until now. The time it took him to count was all the time I got before this trader decided my fate. "Take her back to headquarters. The Xaolin will pay the rest." That's when the second trap sprung.

My smoke bomb canisters burst through the windows, one after another. Smoke filled the room in seconds.

The lead thug, our "informant," grabbed me again and pressed his cannon to my head.

"Call them off," he growled at me.

Call who off? Why? What was my incentive again? He had just promised to give me to people who would kill me on sight. Why would I call off anything? He pulled my hair and clamped his hand around my throat. No chance to catch a breath before I started to choke. "Stop them," he said again, like I knew what was going on.

"I will kill her. Stop!"

The response? More canisters. Four more. The last one landed right at my feet. It wasn't smoke. I couldn't tell what it was until it burst.

It was a static discharge bomb.

The floor pulsed, electric arcs everywhere. Every arm cannon in the room shorted and fried on the spot, including the one pressed to my head. The guy who was holding me was likely in neural shock. His hand kept tightening around my neck in convulsive spasms. If he were stronger, I'd be dead.

That's not to say the blast had no effect. My Aquian genes protected me, but I could feel the surge of electrical energy pulse through me. My head was spinning, my vision swimming in disarray. I was so cold I thought I was dying. It felt like a wave of ice pushing through my entire nervous system. That's why Mom said artificial energy doesn't feel right.

A moment later, my captor passed out and I collapsed to the ground.

Couldn't move.
Couldn't breathe.
Hyperventilating.

The air tasted like burning copper.

Then I felt a hand. Familiar. It was **his** hand.

"Time to go, sis."

Alley pulled me up. The room was chaos: smoke, flame, shouting, cannonfire, and none of it from our captors. I couldn't see a single face. He led me to the window, stopping me just before it. He held me tighter.

"You better let me go first." He spun me around and dove backward out the window, pulling me out with him.

He took the landing. I know he did. I hit the ground hard, but not as hard as I should've.

He got me up and pulled me along. We ran. Past the alleys. Past the market. Into the trees. We didn't stop until the city was just a bruise on the horizon.

We're in the woods now. Somewhere outside the outpost. I don't know where.

When we were finally safe, it was like the floodgates opened. I didn't even feel it at first. I collapsed into his arms. I didn't realize I was crying until I felt the moisture on his shirt.

He's resting now. I bandaged him the best I could. His back took the worst of the fall, along with his side and ribs. He's in bad shape.

I keep replaying everything. Every second. Every word. What did I do wrong?

I asked him why we didn't go back to the ship. He said his parents are gone. They flew out deliberately, created a distraction, drew all the attention.

Wait... was that the plan? To send Alley into a room full of armed assailants just to get me out? Who agrees to that? Who risks their kid for that? He said his folks had him covered and that he was small enough to sneak in unseen. They bought him time. They put him in danger.

When I asked why, he said he volunteered. Aunt Linda was going to do it, but he admitted she's the better shot and has the better arm. Alley said he's better up close and personal. I know he was bragging. He even threw in a flex. He wanted me to laugh, and I pretended to. I can't. I never knew who I had in my corner.

We're not safe. We're barely alive. The whole outpost will be hunting us by morning.

Right now, I'm just staring at Alley. He's asleep in the dirt, ribs bruised, bleeding a little, and still breathing steady. Even when I turn my back, he's still watching me. Still making sure I'm alright, when he's not.

This is what it means to be trained for this. To be raised by warriors.

I think I'm starting to understand what it really means... to be someone who survives. If he, if they, are willing to do all that for me... I guess we really are family.

Diary Entry # 46 – Cost of Survival

A.T. 269, Month 4, Day 18 (Voltaire Standard Time)

Short entry today. I feel like I'm overreacting. Maybe I'm not.

I tried to withdraw money this morning, just enough for food. The account was locked. It had to be Mom. Some kind of failsafe she built in. I should've expected it. Still... that single denial felt like a door slamming shut. We didn't stay in town long. Too many faces from the outpost. Too many stares.

On our way out, Alley stole food. I tried to stop him. He didn't even look at me. Just said, "We need it," and kept walking.

I made a note of the name of the place. Even the brand on the packaging. I'll pay them back. Somehow. Every credit, plus interest. It's the only way I can live with this.

I didn't eat. Couldn't. It wasn't the food, not even the stealing. It was what it meant... what I'd have to admit by eating it. Admitting that we're really in this deep. That we've become people who steal to survive. That scared me more than I want to admit.

Alley noticed, of course. He always notices. He didn't yell. Not then. He just gave me that tired look, like he was holding something in.

Vault Diary - Hypothesis Oblivion

We've been walking for days now, town to town. Alley's quiet. Not like before. His focus is tighter, colder, like he's conserving energy, saving it for when we'll really need it.

I keep wondering how he does it. How he stays calm, sharp, still looking after me when the world is literally hunting us. I asked him that. He didn't answer.

Tonight, he cracked.

We found a quiet spot in the middle of nowhere. Built a small fire. He cooked something... I don't even know when he stole it. He handed me a piece. "Eat."

I shook my head.

That's when it happened.

He didn't shout. His voice wasn't angry; it was desperate. He took my hands and looked me in the eye.

"You need your strength," he said. "I need your strength. If you stop, we die. This isn't about what's right. It's survival. You wrote down the name. Great. You can pay them back when we get out of this. Right now, Maria, you have to eat."

I don't know why that broke me. Maybe it was because he said he needed me. No one says that to me. Not like that. Not without an agenda, or a correction, or a follow-up about what I'm doing wrong. He wasn't wrong either. I was weak. I hadn't eaten in nearly three days.

I ate.

My stomach is full, but everything else inside me feels sick. I'm starting to forget who I was. I'm not sure who that makes me now.

I want to believe I'm still a good person. What does that even mean here? What good is doing the right thing if the price is always paid in someone else's blood? If that's the world I live in... when exactly am I allowed to stop doing the right thing? Who's left when I sacrifice that? Is it gone forever?

We need off this planet while there is still something of me left.

Diary Update:

Alley says there's a rendezvous point. We'll meet up with Uncle Quince and Aunt Linda tomorrow. The nightmare might be ending. Or maybe it's just about to change shape.

I wish I knew which.

Vault Diary - Hypothesis Oblivion

Diary Entry # 47 – When the Anchor Starts to Drift

A.T. 269, Month 4, Day 21 (Voltaire Standard Time)

I'm barely holding on. I think Alley's letting go.

We made it to the rendezvous point two days ago. We stayed low, watched the skies, and waited. From dawn until dusk. Every passing hour dragged like a lifetime.

I tried to breathe slowly, evenly, like Aunt Linda taught me. Four counts in, six counts out. But try doing that for an entire day. I think I permanently broke my lungs. Then they came. Not Uncle Quince. Not Aunt Linda.

Strangers. Not locals. You could tell from how they moved, too careful, too focused. They were looking for something. Or someone. We didn't move or speak. Most of them were very cautious, kept to the shadows, which was itself a tell, but two were careless. I saw it. Not just any blade. The dagger. The same curved sickle design from my room.

I froze. My vision narrowed. My heart jumped so high in my chest it tried to escape through my mouth. Alley had to cover it with his hand, keeping the scream in by sheer force of will.

When the guy was finally gone and my throat unlocked, I whispered, *"That was one of them."*

His answer was quiet. *"I know."*

I told him, *"We have to go."*

He said, *"No."* He didn't even look at me.

He kept watching.

I watched him. The lines in his face grew sharper. His shoulders tightened. His certainty cracked, almost shattered like tempered glass, held together only by the form of what once was. I saw panic creep in, slow and silent like smoke under a door. He tried to pretend it wasn't there. It was all he had.

That was the hardest part. Seeing him, Alley—the one who never breaks—start to fold under it all. As the stars appeared, I leaned close again and whispered, *"We have to go."*

He nodded. *"Tomorrow. They'll come tomorrow. They have to."*

He didn't believe it. Not really. I think he needed to say it out loud, the last comfort of a meaningless lie.

Truth is, after two days he knows we have to move on. Come back in a week, after the heat dies down. Alley himself said that was protocol. I don't think he's going to survive protocol.

We left after midnight. Quiet, careful, invisible. I managed to grab a map on the way out. (Might've stolen it. The display didn't say it was for sale. Let's call it ambiguous ownership.)

We walked until our feet stopped feeling like feet. I studied the map until my eyes burned my eyelids shut. By then, the map was practically a new lobe in my brain. I don't know if I slept when I finally closed my eyes.

I know the thought that woke me up. I realized... there is a way off this planet. No credits. No help. Just risk. Serious risk. The kind of risk that lands you in a prison colony. A prison sentence still means you're alive, right?

I haven't told Alley yet. He's not himself. He hasn't said more than a few words since we left the town. I think he's shutting down.

He always tells me I'm the one who overthinks things. The one who spirals.

He's quiet now. Too still. For the first time since this whole thing started... I'm the one thinking straight. If he can't lead us out of this... I will. I have to. I owe that to him.

Diary Entry # 48 – Oxygen and Silence

A.T. 269, Month 4, Day 60 (Galactic Standard Time)

I never thought I'd be grateful for all those times Dad dragged me around remote bases.

Every meeting. Every protocol rundown. Every diagram of ships and processing stations. I hated it then. Would've rather been anywhere else. But now? That stuff is saving our lives.

There's one army facility on Voltaire III. Not a major base, just a minor outpost, mostly for waste processing. Fitting, I guess. No offense to the waste.

Security was light. We still had to hop a fence and dodge patrols, but after everything we've been through, it was barely a challenge. Honestly, the scariest part was wondering if Alley's jump over the fence would make a clang loud enough to wake the whole station.

We weren't there for the garbage. We slipped into the refitting sector instead. Quiet. Low activity.

It took a few minutes of searching ships before we found it, our ride. A transport shuttle, already staged for automated loading. They had just finished inspection. It was perfect. Small enough not to need a pilot, just programmed to fly cargo to another site.

We climbed in through the cargo hold. I'm not exaggerating when I say it was the tightest squeeze of my life. There was barely room to breathe. If the hold had been airtight, we would've died.

Alley and I had to fit facing each other, forehead to forehead at first, and then somehow... cheek to cheek. Way too close. Not a kiss, just two fugitives sharing oxygen and regret. Every time I moved, I elbowed his ribs. He had the gall to joke about the *"cozy ambiance."*

If I ever see a ventilation shaft or a cargo hold again, I'm going to scream. We waited in the dark. Pitch black. No sound except each other's breathing and the faint hum of machinery.

Eventually, we felt the floor shift. The sound of clamps locking. The slow rattle of lift-off.

That's when we knew we were in the air.

We opened the door to the rest of the cargo bay. Carefully. Quietly. We had the whole transport to ourselves. No guards. No crew. No cameras. Two days of quiet.

It feels unnatural to be safe. No wake-up calls with knives. No panic attacks. No holding my breath because a wrong move might kill us both.

Yet... I can't relax. Not really. The silence is too loud, like pressure building in a sealed tank. You don't hear it until it bursts.

Alley's been quiet too. Not broken. Not the ghost he was a few days ago. He made a dumb joke earlier about how cramped cargo holds are the *"premier travel experience."* He smiled. Not a big one, but enough to count.

He's coming back to himself, bit by bit. There's still exhaustion in his eyes, but he's watching again, scanning, thinking, planning. It's a relief.

The thing is... I'm not. I don't know what comes next. I got us off-planet. I played my hand. I'm out of cards.

Mom's still missing. Aunt Linda and Uncle Quince are gone. We don't even know who's behind this, or why. For now, we're floating. Literally and metaphorically.

I've never been so glad to be nowhere.

Vault Diary - Hypothesis Oblivion

Diary Entry # 49 – Hope in the Scrap

A.T. 269, Month 4, Day 63 (Galactic Standard Time)

Turns out this transport is split between two types of cargo: one set to be refitted, the other to be burned.

It's not the most efficient system. Then again, I never accused the Army of resource optimization. Sorry, Dad.

It took a while to find the condemned cargo.

Alley was livid that I even suggested we only scavenge from that section. He doesn't understand. Yes, I'm brave enough to bum a ride on a military transport. Steal from them? Absolutely not. I'm desperate, not suicidal.

Everything in the condemned section is scheduled for destruction, which makes it fair game. There's actual law to back that up. I still remember Dad ranting once about someone *"liberating"* a decommissioned sensor array from his hangar. (You really think I'm the first person to think of this?)

Alley found some expired rations in a damaged container. Not great. Not awful. But food. Weeks' worth, in fact. Somehow, eating something that tastes like cardboard feels better than eating something stolen.

While he inventoried supplies, I tore apart five broken devices to cobble together a rudimentary scanner. Then I put them all back together. (I'll take my gold star now.)

It worked. I have a heading, and I found a star chart to confirm it. We're headed to Foretto.

It's a long shot, a long way from home… but it's the first good news we've had in weeks.

Mom has a friend there. He's insufferable, pompous, and probably the most obnoxious person I've ever met. He adores my mother. Always has. So much that Dad hated him for years and even kicked him out once. Mom and her friend served together, both Inquisitors once. Now he's a prince. Literally.

Powerful enough that the Xaolin wouldn't dare touch him. Hopefully. If we can get to him, he can help us. That's a big if, but it's a start.

Alley… isn't okay. He tries to act like he is. He jokes. He spars. He hums when he thinks I'm not listening. I catch him more and more, standing at the viewport, staring at the stars. He's not looking at them. He's searching. For his mom and dad.

He asked me today if I could build a communicator strong enough to reach them. A signal. A sign. Anything. Not with what we have. Not out here.

I told him he didn't have to hold up some front for me. I know how he feels. I'm terrified. I miss my folks too. He insisted we have a productive mindset, admitted he was scared, and said not to worry. He'd take care of me, as long as it takes.

I told him everything was going to be okay.

"You don't know that."

"I know."

We both knew it was a lie. We clung to it anyway. The weird thing is… it helped.

Sometimes, a lie in the dark is its own kind of truth, not because it's real, but because it holds you together for one more day.

I don't know if everything will be okay. I have hope. Maybe that's enough.

Alley and I have sat here for the last few hours, staring out the window. He's finally gone to sleep. He held me this whole time. It was like being with my father, except I saw him crying when he thought I wasn't looking. No noise. No mess. He didn't bother to wipe his eyes. Just glared ahead as though he was angry at his tears.

When he finally nodded off, I dried his eyes.

Story 008: Carmen Foretto

Girls often dream of being a princess or a queen. Why? What makes royalty desirable? For every privilege, there's a poison. Power brings responsibility and a target marker. Beauty brings intrusion and the sting of degeneration. Money brings complacency and the temptation of excess.

Mom was rich, but she never let me live like royalty. I knew I would inherit it all one day, me, the reluctant princess. That day meant my parents were gone. That's all I ever saw in wealth: a lonely dungeon. No amount of money is worth that.

My mother was always the Queen. She was trapped in her performance, loud hats, flowing gowns, and a constant act. No thank you. Even as an adult trapped in a child's frame, I knew I'd rather be myself.

It's just hard... when you're still not sure who *yourself* is.

In that sense, I guess Carmen was my first role model.

Vault Diary - Hypothesis Oblivion

Diary Entry # 50 – Foretto

A.T. 269, Month 4, Day 17 (Forettian Standard Time)

Breaking out of a military facility is harder than breaking in, especially with a thirteen-year-old limping beside you and a backpack full of stolen protein bars. A calculated risk. Somehow, it worked.

Alley's taller than most kids his age, tall enough to pass for a young recruit. Our transport had no shortage of discarded uniforms and a few pieces of civilian clothes. Good thing too. By this point I've been wearing the same clothes for almost a week... gross.

I posed as his daughter. He straightened his back, dropped his voice, and barked orders like he'd been born on a parade ground. Disturbingly effective. Maybe he missed his calling. My short stint as Alley's daughter lands somewhere in my top ten bizarre moments. He yelled at me for talking back and, for a second, I swear I was talking to my mother.

My father has a presence that says, *"Try it... and DIE."*

It took us a full day on foot to reach the capital. It might have taken half as long, but the last week took something out of Alley. He could only make himself eat two protein bars. I could only manage one myself. Something about the texture was off.

Some of the spoiled bars had worms inside, helping themselves since the army didn't bother. I swear I felt a constant tingle in my stomach for the rest of the day. Did I eat worm larvae? Probably not, but I wanted to throw up.

Either way, we made it to Foretto. Okay, with these people you have to be specific. We made it to the capital city, Foretto. (Seriously, why is the city named the same as the planet? Did they run out of creativity that day? To be fair, Kameon C's capital is Kameon Centrum, so maybe it's a naming convention.)

First stop: the bank. I was able to access our emergency funds and send compensation for everything Alley and I "borrowed" over the last few weeks. We couldn't exactly knock on the palace door and ask for an audience with the Prince. Fortunately, I remembered what Mom said: he's got a favorite lounge he visits when he wants to *"be seen."* I made sure I was there. It took a couple of hours before he arrived, but he noticed me instantly.

Foretto — the man, not the planet. What can I say about him? Carmen Foretto is exactly the hurricane of obnoxious charisma he always was. Loud. Bright. Flamboyant. Stylish to a level that should be illegal. He was so happy to see me I thought he might lift me off the ground. He already knew about the attack on our family. He had talked to Mom five days ago, Forettian Time.

"Your mom follows the hit men, I follow the money. If I can find the client who paid them... the client's assets vanish. Quietly. Permanently. Problem solved. I've yet to find a knife that stabs for free."

He didn't say it like a maybe. The plan was already in motion. I'd swear an errant synapse in his brain actually enjoyed this, somewhere between a predator savoring the hunt and a showman mid-performance.

I asked about it, and he insists he's not an Inquisitor anymore, but *"being a prince has its advantages."*

What he didn't know was where Mom had gone, or if she was still alive. He insisted that *"being light with details is what keeps us alive."* He said he would put out a call to his sources, informants, and inquisitors. Mom would be using the same people. If she's out there, he'll find her.

I could have hugged him, flaming-loud red cape and all.

He took us in like we were his own blood. Got us to a hospital. I did eat worm larvae. Eww.

He fed us like we'd just returned from war. Let me tell you, watching one man inhale six plates of food while Alley tried to match him bite for bite was an experience I never want to relive. Alley threw up less than ten minutes later. *"Totally worth it,"* he said.

Now I'm sitting in a room with velvet curtains, silk pajamas, and a mattress softer than my conscience. Alley's in the room across the hall, just as awkward in his borrowed finery. It's hard to eat in silk pajamas knowing Mom might be bleeding in a ditch somewhere. For once, I don't feel like the only one who doesn't belong.

Carmen's already contacted Dad. He knows we're safe. Told us to stay put.

I can't sleep. My ghosts have returned, and I'm having horror books play out in full view all night, every night. I went across the hall to check on Alley. He's having nightmares too now. Crying in his sleep. Calling for his mom. I want to wake him. I want to scream. I can't do either.

Instead, I hold him and dry his tears. He seems to calm down a bit when I do. Instead, I'm writing this. We have to find our parents. If we don't find a way to help, this palace is just a prison.

Vault Diary - Hypothesis Oblivion

Diary Entry # 51 – The Knife

A.T. 269, Month 4, Day 18 (Forettian Standard Time)

I saw the knife again today. One day, maybe, I'll be able to look at one without breaking into a sweat, a full-body panic. Not today.

Let's start at the beginning. I don't know how much longer Alley is going to hold together. He's unraveling. Not completely, but the cracks are widening. He's either in the gym beating himself up or in the palace comm center, trying to reach his parents. Today he finally got a response from Strand, whoever that is. His message:

Our parents are alive. The hit is still active.

He ran straight to me. Found me locked in my room, just finished a therapy session Carmen insisted on after I told him everything. (For once, I didn't argue.) When I opened the door and saw Alley, I nearly collapsed from the look on his face. I wasn't ready for more bad news.

When I came out, Alley was pacing. Frantic. He dragged me to the throne room to see Carmen. Asked for a ship. Denied. Asked for weapons. Denied. I get it. He wants to do something. Right now... we're caged.

Carmen sent Alley to train with the Royal Guard to burn energy and learn discipline. He sent me to wait for a scheduled secure call with Dad. I wasn't thrilled, but it meant I'd finally get answers. I barely made it out of the throne room before it happened.

I saw it. Saw him, at the opposite end of the hall.

The Knife.

Not just any knife. A Xaolin sickle dagger. The same kind used in the first attack. Strapped to the belt of a man casually walking the palace halls. Panic hit me like a wall. Hyperventilating. Trembling. Five minutes, maybe more. When the shaking stopped, he was still there. Still laughing with one of Carmen's chefs.

I don't know what possessed me to do it, but I followed him.

Kept my distance. Watched. He didn't look back once. He's in Room 317. Staying here. In our palace.

By the time I pulled myself away, I'd missed the call. I almost didn't care.

I stumbled toward the training grounds and found Alley with the Guard. He saw my face before I said a word. I told him everything. My first thought: tell Carmen. Get security. Lock down the palace. Alley had a different idea. Not better. Just... dangerous.

"What if we track him?" he asked. At first I said no.

"You want to find our parents? Find out who is trying to kill us?" Maybe for the first time in my life, logic got into a fight with mortal dread... and won. To be fair, I trembled even though I agreed. If this guy's part of the same Xaolin cell, he might have tech — some kind of device, comms gear, locator chip. If I can isolate the signature, maybe I can trace who sent them, find why.

So now we're watching. Sleeping in shifts. I'm up first. Alley's asleep. Face half-lit by the monitors. Arms curled around a throw pillow like it's a riot shield. He looks peaceful for once. Calm, at ease, no tears.

I wish I knew what peace felt like, but this is worth it—if only to give Alley his. That alone lets me rest a little easier.

Diary Entry # 52 – Smoke and Science

A.T. 269, Month 4, Day 21 (Forettian Standard Time)

Maybe my true calling is spy work. Or Inquisitor. Okay, I'm being dramatic, but today felt like a thriller: all recon, all tension, the most alive I've felt in weeks.

We've been tailing the Xaolin operative, Nenyok Lovett, for the past three days. At first, I thought he spotted me. His eyes flicked my way once. No reaction. Still, too close. I changed tactics.

Aquians don't blend in. Brown skin, white hair? It's like a neon sign. So I covered everything. Black robe, hood, silver synth gloves to pass for Kameonic. I looked like a haunted monk. Alley, of course, wore his usual outfit. Somehow, he always fits in.

I rigged up a short-range radio system. He was my eyes on the street. I monitored signals and patterns. It worked.

We learned Lovett never strays far from his room unless he's carrying something. A sack. Big. Heavy.

Why?

Alley picked the lock while he was gone. (Actually, we broke in a couple of times. He was way too comfortable doing it too.) We didn't touch anything. Just looked. We saw enough. This guy's hiding something. Every time he leaves with his bag, the room is spotless. Not clean, empty. Like he moves out every time he steps away.

His official story? He's a dignitary from Voltaire III. We just came from Voltaire III, and they are NOT sending dignitaries to Foretto. The place has no intergalactic ties. The only reason there's an army base there is that it's the cheapest land between Kameon C and the Pyrosia incinerator facility.

Carmen says he's been cleared. I've seen enough *"cleared"* people to know when they're dirty. There's nothing dignified about this man's movements. Alley thinks there's a hit on someone here.

Not us. Someone else. Honestly? That makes sense. Lovett's behavior isn't predator mode. It's *recon*.

Can we catch him before he catches anyone else?

Alley asked if I could think of a way to search the room without him knowing. I didn't answer right away. I could think of a way. I just hated it.

My first instinct was fear. I could use biochemistry. That's how I nearly killed people. That's how I lost myself. I still see Jenkave in my nightmares, a strange, guardian-angel kind of ghost. He helps when the other ghosts are too much. I know I killed him; I'd rather face those demons than rely on him, but I do.

Alley didn't push. He just said, *"Let's get you a lab."* He went to Carmen himself and said I needed a workspace. Alley never even had to say why. Apparently word of my science experiments traveled faster than I did. All the things I built. I've only been doing this for months. How did he know so much? Carmen handed over the keys to the royal lab on one condition: he gets a front-row seat to my little *science fair.* That was the price. Carmen gets a demo. I get to fight my ghosts.

I'm back in the lab, in a white coat, staring at a board and a pile of reagents like they're boobytrapped. Can I make a compound that knocks Lovett out just long enough to check his gear? Yes, maybe. Do I trust myself not to make another fatal mistake? That's the harder question. The simple answer is not yet. I told Alley I was terrified. He didn't give a speech. Didn't promise it would be fine. He just said, *"You're not that girl anymore."*

I hope he's right. I'm trying, Alley.

I promise I'm trying.

Vault Diary - Hypothesis Oblivion

Diary Entry # 53 – The Coat and the Needle

A.T. 269, Month 4, Day 22 (Forettian Standard Time)

This morning, an aqua-blue lab coat hung on my door with a note:

"See you in the lab. Quickly, Doctor. Time is short."

I stared at it for ten minutes. I told myself I gave that life up. Then I saw my Mom in my mind, ducking behind cover, running recon, risking everything just to uncover the truth. She gave up that life too. I never knew the Inquisitor, but if she could go back...

I put it on. The uniform: lab coat, hooded cloak, silver gloves. Time to work.

When I stepped out of my room, I ran straight into him. Lovett. The one we've been watching. Face to face. He didn't strike. He just looked me over, his hand hovering a little too close to that sickle blade.

"Do you work here?" he asked.

What? I was ready for a knife to the throat, a threat, a death sentence, not small talk. I forced the stutter out of my *"No,"* and added something about being late. It always works for Mom when she's at the tax office. He stepped aside. I sprinted down the hall, heart pounding so loud it felt like footsteps.

I didn't stop until I reached the lab. There I collapsed. Full panic. On the floor. Shaking. Sobbing.

Alley barricaded the door, then held me through the whole thing, freaking out for a second before it descended into just confusion. I was too shaken to tell him anything. He knew we weren't in danger, and I guess that was enough. It felt like forever. Twenty-three minutes and twelve seconds.

When my brain finally returned, panic rewrote the plan in an instant, like a neuron firing in reverse. *"Yeah,"* I muttered. *"You're not fighting that guy."*

We're going to put him to sleep via aerosol. I gulped looking at the vials and beakers all around. It's no longer good enough to have a proper chemical mix. Now I need a delivery system that's effective at range.

I spent three hours mixing. I almost had a catastrophic spill; forgot my lab safeguards book at home. Still, the end product? A chemical sedative with rapid dispersion. Delivers through aerosol from a pressurized capsule. The mechanism fits a slim shaft, short enough to slide under a door and knock out a grown man in two seconds flat.

We'll have an hour of unconsciousness, minimum.

I insisted on testing it on myself. If my mixture was wrong, I'd spend a week in the hospital wing. I went over what to do if there was a mistake with Alley ten times. He volunteered five of those times to be the test subject until I started yelling at him. He eventually agreed that he could get me to the hospital fastest, and that was that.

The test was uneventful, or so it seemed. One second I was pressing my hand to the door. Next, I woke up in bed.

Apparently, I stood for almost five seconds before collapsing. Didn't twitch. Didn't dream. Mechanical shutdown. It might be the best sleep I've had since this whole nightmare started.

Alley insists on delivering the real dose tomorrow morning, at precisely 6:00 A.M. Our Xaolin friend wakes at that time every day.

I know the theory works. What I don't know, what I can't know, is what we'll find when we open that door. I have to know what this person has. What he's up to.

I still have a hard time trusting myself. I see all the ways that things can go wrong. My mind keeps creating disaster scenarios, the worst being I somehow kill this guy. That said, I have to do this. I have to believe that I am still capable of stepping up in this way. If I can't trust the mind that made this, then maybe I really did leave it all behind.

Now? I think I want it back.

Diary Entry # 54 – Five Seconds

A.T. 269, Month 4, Day 22 (Forettian Standard Time)

We struck today. Five-second window. That's all we had.

The plan: Alley waits by the door with the delivery stick prepped on our side. When the target approaches from inside, we wait for the rustle of movement, then slide the device under just as he opens the door.

Smoothest operation of my life. Alley walked by like he was just passing through, slid the stick under with his shoe, and knocked once. Steam hissed under the door. Thud. Three seconds.

The door was ajar. We slipped in.

Xaolin Lovett was unconscious, barely breathing. We dragged him to the bed. Alley redressed him in pajamas (how that became his job, I don't know), while I raided the room.

His gear was military-grade. Xaolin tech mirrors army systems almost exactly, probably because so many Xaolin are ex-army.

I cloned his drive. Thanks to my crash course in computer systems — thanks, Mom — I was able to start decrypting immediately.

What I found was worse than we thought. Surveillance footage of the throne room, the dining room. Every space Carmen spends time in. For a second I thought Alley and I were the target. We kept popping up in the footage. But he's bumped into me in the halls, armed, alone, just us, and did nothing. He doesn't even know who we are.

The Xaolin data network must be decentralized. Makes sense. Capture one, and you get nothing except information on the mission they're on.

Then, in his bag, a vial. Small. Unlabeled. I took a sample for study.

He had an entire wardrobe of royal house uniforms. Guard, liaison, servant, chef—nearly every position in the castle was in his bag. This guy's a chameleon. He could be anyone, anytime.

It didn't take long to decode the data. Xaolin cryptographers should be fired. Two hours, and there it was.

Target: Prince Carmen Foretto.

Method: Poison.

Here's the twist: the poison isn't lethal. At least, not to most people. The compound is biochemically stable; in most species across the galaxy, it would cause nothing worse than mild indigestion.

Not for Carmen.

His body lacks the enzyme to break it down, so Vicantine Floralite converts into a toxic metabolite called Vicantine Floral Acid. In his case, a normal exposure turns into a runaway reaction. The metabolite builds up faster than his system can clear it. The result is a megadose of toxin, fast and lethal.

The only reason I know is because of my mother. She told me once, laughing about Carmen's ridiculous allergy while planning a menu. She loves him. She would never forget.

I ran. Grabbed my data stick and bolted from the lab. Alley tore after me, shouting for me to stop. There was no way Carmen would believe me.

But I had to try.

I found him and burst into the room. He was in full uniform, immaculate, surrounded by dignitaries, his father the King leading the meeting. The scene gave me flashbacks to the space station with Dad. Same tension, same politics. It was déjà vu in every sense, except the reaction was completely different.

He didn't tune me out. He stood, cut the meeting short, and dismissed the dignitaries, dramatic and decisive. His father blinked, his glare caught somewhere between confusion and resignation, then followed the delegation out. For a moment, the palace felt like it belonged to someone else— not a king, but a performer who could command the room.

Alley and I just watched, stunned. Carmen had the showmanship and the power to clear the hall, but I wasn't sure showmanship alone would save him.

The moment the last dignitary left, he grabbed his flashiest red cape and swung it over his shoulders. He was back to himself in all his flaming glory.

"Now, tell me what you've found, little ruby."

What did he just call me? I would have objected if I wasn't so disoriented. It wasn't just the threat to his life; his reactions made it worse. I told him everything. He sighed and rolled his eyes.

"That jerk."

Alley looked like he'd swallowed a battery. I admit I felt the same. I just told Carmen an assassin was trying to kill him, and he acted like someone ate the last slice of his favorite pie. Even when he asked for details, it sounded like he was catching up on the latest gossip.

Carmen listened to the whole story from start to finish. He studied the sample and read the files.

Then he said, "Good work. We'll handle it from here. Knowledge is the best defense."

That was it. No panic. No guards. No lockdown. Just Carmen being Carmen: playful, flamboyant, calm, like this was only another costume change. He didn't dismiss me the way I'm used to seeing adults do, but he didn't seem to take it seriously either.

I am not okay. This man is going to die if we don't stop it. He doesn't grasp how dangerous this is. He might be a flagrant idiot, but I have to save him. My own father shut the door in my face. Carmen opened it wide, cleared the room, and asked what I knew. I know he believes me; I just think he underestimates them. It is amazing, though, to have someone not underestimate me.

I've been up all night working through the rest of the drive, trying to map movements, cross-check the security feed, and reconstruct his full operation.

There's more here. More than poison. More than Carmen. I feel it. Somewhere in that data is the next piece. If I fail here, it's not just Carmen who will die.

Vault Diary - Hypothesis Oblivion

Diary Entry # 55 – Checkmate

A.T. 269, Month 4, Day 24 (Forettian Standard Time)

Lovett struck tonight at dinner. A banquet, actually, hosted by Carmen. I didn't want to go, but Carmen didn't exactly ask. He presented Alley and me with tailored outfits and declared it "a gift from the House of Foretto."

Alley looked like someone kicked his soul. He had to wear the royal house colors because, and I quote, "he would stand in for my son Carisi, who's away at boarding school."

Alley tried to refuse. I convinced him to suffer the embarrassment just in case Lovett made a move. He looked like a royal clown.

"Yeah, no one's gonna recognize me in this getup," he grumbled —depressed, at least until right before dinner.

We were called to the royal comm center. Guess who was on the screen? Aunt Linda. Uncle Quince.

I think they laughed harder than I did when they saw Alley in formal wear. Uncle Quince couldn't breathe for a full five seconds. Alley was so happy to see them he didn't even care. In fact, he laughed too. I tried to sneak out to give Alley his time with his parents, but he insisted I stay.

The reunion was brief. They went back to Voltaire III the very day we left to try to find us. Carmen got word to them that we were safe via my dad. They'd been hiding in a nebula behind an asteroid belt near a pair of moons, spending days dodging patrols and running on fumes.

"If our engines weren't tuned to perfection, we would have never escaped."

My work helped. I know that was what Uncle Quince meant. I felt that, and I needed it more than I'm comfortable admitting.

Aunt Linda seemed the most at ease. She told us to stay put. They said they'd meet up with us soon. They've found my mom. She's alive. They're seeing her tomorrow.

We didn't tell them about Lovett. We didn't have a chance. They had to cut the signal before someone could intercept the communication and find them. Alley was so much better after that.

At dinner, Lovett made his move. I didn't see the exact moment, but I know he spiked Carmen's drink. A toast was called to "the health of the king." The way Lovett watched Carmen told me everything. That was the trap. I tried to stop Carmen, to warn him.

He winked at me, then downed his entire glass in one gulp.

I nearly passed out. Everyone clapped. Everyone drank.

Except Lovett. He stared, locked in, waiting for it to take hold. He had nailed his shot and only needed to confirm the kill.

A minute later, Carmen collapsed face-first into his plate. Gasps. Screams. I froze. Lovett ran. Alley sprang into action, circling the table the opposite way to block the door.

Lovett never made it that far.

Guards tackled him, four of them. They pinned him down and dragged him back. Alley stopped in his tracks.

Carmen sat up.

He wiped his mouth, grinned like a showman, and laughed.

"Thanks, kids."

He held up a vial of liquid, unstoppered it, and dropped a drip into his own glass, then into several others.

His drink turned bright blue. The others stayed clear.

"Vicantine Floralite," he said, examining the glow. "Very clever."

Then he turned and poured the rest of the vial over Lovett's hands. His skin bloomed blue, like a flower.

"Would've worked if I hadn't taken my enzyme tablets. Bested by children."

His smile vanished.

"Get this scum out of my sight. And find out who he works for."

Just like that. Checkmate.

Carmen handed us Lovett's bag from the closet along with the key to his room. He gave us full access to his materials. "Anything you can find," he said, "is yours to use." The room itself was useless, but the bag was a treasure trove: encoded orders, communications keys, target lists.

We've started decoding. More Xaolin will come, for Carmen and for us.

Foretto isn't safe anymore. Carmen has to disappear. If we want to stay ahead of the Xaolin, we do too.

Diary Entry # 56 – Return Vector

A.T. 269, Month 4, Day 100 (Galactic Standard Time)

I did it. I finally did it. I cracked the Xaolin comm frequency.

I can hear their transmissions, track them, trace them. That means I can follow their movements and maybe, just maybe, figure out who's giving them orders.

We couldn't sit still, and surprisingly, neither could Carmen. When we told him the Xaolin were still coming for us, he didn't hesitate. He called Dad himself.

Dad agreed. He sent Vaughn to extract us. Safehouse ready. On Tula. I never thought I'd feel conflicted about going home.

Packing was harder than I expected. Carmen gave us both a "reasonably normal" wardrobe to travel with. I kept stopping in the middle of folding things, staring at the walls. Not really sure how to explain it. Maybe because I'm going back to a place that doesn't have Mom in it.

That's when Alley noticed.

"You're wearing your lab coat," he said. I looked down. I was. Not in the lab, not on assignment. Just wearing it. Like I used to.

"Good to have you back."

Before I could respond, Carmen swept into the room, flamboyant and glowing, back to his usual *self-induced solar flare* form. He praised us, of course. Told us we had his respect—like we didn't already know. Then he asked if I wanted to meet his son.

He suggested that a Foretto–Maze alliance might "serve the galaxy well." He has my ultimate respect. Join his family? Hard no.

I made up some excuse, internally barfed, and externally smiled. He did take us in, after all.

After he left, I made a joke to Alley about what kind of son a man like that must be raising. He snorted and laughed, then called me "Mistress Foretto." I backhanded him in the gut. Anyone else would have gotten a punch in the face. Blasphemy.

Carmen interrupted us. Vaughn had arrived. I thanked him. Really thanked him. Then I asked if he would tell us a story before we left. His stories were always my favorite thing about Uncle Carmen. He told us one. Alley was surprised, but I sat back to enjoy it.

He told the most ridiculous story about how he once accidentally prevented a war by seducing a general's pet and stealing the peace treaty. There was a smirk across his face the whole time. I didn't believe a word, but I loved every second. At the end, he showed me a picture of an almost equally flamboyantly dressed woman. She looked regal, fancy, wild, and happy. I had never seen anyone more alive in their own brand of crazy. I guess it's true.

Vault Diary - Hypothesis Oblivion

When it was over, Vaughn was standing at attention by the door. It was the very definition of contrast captured in a single image: military precision and quiet discipline against flair and royalty. Vaughn all but ignored Carmen, insisting he take us to our ship. Any deference to his majesty was gone. Carmen didn't seem to care. He invited Alley and me to come back anytime as guests of the royal family.

I can't believe I'm saying this, but I'll miss him.

Alley nudged me when he was out of earshot. "I get why you like him now. Me too."

On the ship, Vaughn handed us rations. They tasted like dust after a week of palace feasts. He made a halfhearted attempt to recruit Alley. Alley declined violently.

Then Vaughn sat us both down. He told us he was proud, that we had done more than most trained soldiers would have. We are supposed to listen to him now. He is responsible for us.

He gave us a secure line, and we got to talk to all four of our parents. Together. Finally. Mostly together. Dad is still on Kameon Centrum, tracking down leads.

We must have talked for hours. Laughed. Cried. Made plans. We are all going camping when this whole nightmare is over.

I don't remember the call ending, just waking up later. Alley was still asleep, uniform wrinkled. Vaughn, of course, was wide awake. He looked like he had just started his shift.

He motioned for me to sit next to him. We sat quietly for a while, looking out at the endless array of stars.

He asked how I was holding up. "Most girls, heck, most anyone, would have folded. That kind of pressure? That kind of fear? Most people don't make it."

I told him he underestimated girls. We are brilliant survivors. He underestimated kids. We live through what we are given. We survive without power, with nothing but grit.

He agreed. We sat like that for some time, absorbing the silence.

Then I asked, "Will life ever be normal again?" I didn't expect an answer. For the longest time, he didn't give one. He just looked out the window, but I won't forget the answer he finally gave.

"I don't know if life was ever normal. That said, the day will come when you sleep in your own bed, and your biggest worry will be what your mom wants you to do after breakfast tomorrow. When it comes, you'll treasure it more."

I think I believe him. I think I really do.

I don't know what's waiting for us on Tula, but this time, I'm not running from it.

Story 009: The Edge of Normal

One thing I have never understood about Earthlings is that you insist on giving stories themes. Every adventure must prove something, and every struggle must be pressed into a lesson. That strikes me as absurd. When people are trying to kill you, when survival depends on sharp wits, a deep breath, and sometimes a desperate prayer, there is no tidy theme. There is only the choice to endure.

If you demand one, perhaps this will suffice: I lived long enough to discover who I am. That is all the meaning survival ever needed.

I was blessed to find love I did not deserve, from parents, family, and friends. Even those I failed or destroyed became part of that blessing. My ghosts and demons turned into guardians only when I stopped resisting them and began to accept myself, even the parts I once despised. Especially those.

Vault Diary - Hypothesis Oblivion

Diary Entry # 57 – Safehouse Blues

A.T. 269, Month 5, Day 04 (Tulan Standard Time)

I'm trying to do what I'm told here. When we landed, we stayed with Vaughn at a small military outpost on the far side of the Rain Province. Vaughn made omelets with Forettian corn and goat cheese that tasted so much like Aunt Linda's they almost made me cry. Also, Vaughn can cook. Like, really cook. Almost as well as she does. (Almost.)

I asked him once why he never got married. I wasn't ready for the answer.

It turns out he did. He had a wife and a daughter, both died the year before I was born. They were killed in the first Chan raids during the Chan Army War. He was the only one who survived the attack. He joined the army the very next day. My father was his drill sergeant. Vaughn says he is one of the last people Dad ever trained, and he has been following his lead ever since. He was the best man at my parents' wedding. He even bought me my first model set.

I always thought it was from Dad. Apparently, Dad didn't think I'd like it.

Vaughn is uncomfortable with me running scans on Xaolin communications. He lets me do it because I understand the tech better than he does. (Also because he insists on checking everything I build before I plug it in. Paranoid doesn't even begin to cover it.)

Honestly, it feels like I'm on a summer internship for a covert ops division. It would be funny if it didn't also feel real. I analyze, compile, and write intel reports. Alley trains with Vaughn in bladed weapons, short-range combat, and field recovery. I haven't seen him this focused in weeks.

We still talk to our parents every night. They're safe and together, in hiding. Using my scanner, they were able to track down a lead: the person who hired the Xaolin. It might be an army general. That's when Vaughn shut it down. He locked down the location in an hour. We're in a safehouse now, not far from Liviton—quiet, stocked, guarded.

Scanner: confiscated. All data: classified. We were so close to a name. Why freeze us out now? He called Dad as we were being set up. Dad told us not to worry. Said he had a plan. Then he cut off contact with everyone, even the military.

I may have lied. Vaughn doesn't know me well enough to see it yet. Alley caught it immediately. I built a backup receiver. The Xaolin are meeting with their client tomorrow.

Whatever Dad is doing, it's working. Some of the Xaolin targeting high-profile figures are vanishing quietly. My scanner picked up panicked final calls that just cut off mid-sentence. Now they're trying to clean their house before someone finds them.

I'm scared to tell Vaughn. If he confiscates this second receiver, I'm done. It would take me a week with the materials on hand to build another. I told Alley. He said we should check it out ourselves. If we can identify the client, the whole thing ends. The Xaolin only work for pay. No money, no hit.

I know this could get us in trouble, but I think I'm done letting other people decide when I'm allowed to help. We're past "play it safe." If no one else is going to end this, maybe it's time I stop asking permission.

Also, sharing a room with Alley is… strange. Not in the way I expected. It's just like working in the lab. He's oddly meticulous, almost obsessively precise. Certain things have to be exactly where he left them or he gets twitchy. It's like living with a mom. He's a great teammate, steady and reliable, but this space-sharing thing?

Let's just say I miss doors that lock.

Diary Entry # 58 – The General

A.T. 269, Month 5, Day 05 (Tulan Standard Time)

Be careful what you wish for. Alley and I won't be sharing a room again anytime soon.

We slipped out during Vaughn's perimeter check. He's probably figured it out by now. He might be the only reason we survive this.

We tracked the Xaolin meeting to a location in Liviton. In the city. Out in the open. That takes guts, or pure stupidity. The city isn't under army protection, but the Xaolin had their people posted like they owned the place. Maybe they did.

I brought a recording device and transmitter, linked it to the safehouse system, and piped the feed straight to the army emergency channel. Just in case.

We climbed to the roof of the courthouse. That disguise from Foretto has paid for itself. Alley followed me in his own getup. No velos are allowed inside Liviton proper, which still makes me wonder why the Xaolin risked meeting there at all. I guess they needed the space... and the theater.

Their rendezvous spot was a closed-down restaurant just off the square. There were so many of them. At least a hundred, every one armed with sickle daggers, eyes like stone. (Okay, maybe I didn't see all their eyes. But the ones I did? Empty.)

Their plan? Hit the safehouse. They knew exactly where it was. They knew Vaughn was with us. They knew we'd be unguarded. We were supposed to die tonight. They even knew about our Foretto stunt. How could they know so much?

One of the commanders issued orders on the spot: *Proceed with caution. Consider the girl and boy combatants, armed and dangerous.*

Really? Us?

They even reminded each other not to cause collateral damage, as if that made murder sound better. Then he arrived.

Executive General Towelain. Seeing him, everything snapped into place — why my dark matter collector infuriated him, how they could fake a message from my father. That was how they knew where we were tonight. He knew we were no longer on base because of the lockdown. Our protection fell under special operations, and he had access to our files.

What I didn't understand was why he'd want me dead.

Until he spoke:

"Brooks Roamai is coming here. His daughter is here. Perfect bait, but too much like her parents. Too much trouble. She's already ruined our operation with the Forettian government. Carmen and the King are locked down. We can't get to them. Kill the girl, this Maria. Her parents will still fight for the boy. Bring Alejandro to me alive."

Alley and I both froze. I had never hated hearing my name more. We gulped. This man was completely insane.

Before we could react, we heard a voice behind us. Not an assassin. Not a soldier.

A janitor. An actual janitor, mop and bucket and all.

"What are you kids doing up here!?" I think my soul left my body for a second. Why now?

Didn't matter. The damage was done. Suddenly, every Xaolin on the block turned toward us.

No time to think. We ran. Jumped down a fire escape. Sprinted over rooftops. Alley nearly missed one of the jumps. I caught his arm just long enough for him to snag a grip. Longest half-second of my life. My newest ghost will be watching him fall from there, because I saw it a thousand times in that single instant.

Then came the arm cannon bolts. Watching energy bolts fly by, each one meant to incinerate our skulls. My God, I am glad we had cover. The Xaolin were excellent shots. We dove over a vendor cart. Five seconds later, it erupted in flames. The heat licked the back of my neck. How do soldiers survive this? I have a newfound respect for my father.

We vaulted over a crumbling balcony. The weapon blasts were probably our saving grace, masking the sound of our footsteps. By the time they caught up, we were long gone.

Twenty minutes of rooftops and blind alleys. Our lungs were burning. My legs almost gave out.

We finally lost them in the warehouse district near the spaceport.

Now?

We're in a restaurant now, hiding in a cabinet. Yes, an actual cabinet. Crammed between outdated cleaning supplies and what smells like three-year-old engine grease.

I don't know how long we've been here. I just know I'm shaking.

I set the safehouse computer to send out a run signal if we didn't check in by midnight. That was more than two hours ago.

I hope Vaughn got it. I hope he listens. I hope he's okay.

I'm scared. I have the proof. I know who's trying to kill us. If we don't get it out, it means nothing.

Diary Entry # 59 – Jenkave's Rest

A.T. 269, Month 5, Day 06 (Tulan Standard Time)

If I hear one more shield arm cannon blast, I swear my brain will explode, regardless of whether it's aimed at me.

We slipped out of the restaurant right before it opened. The Xaolin had cleared, but I couldn't stop hearing echoes of them in my skull. At least the spaceport had long-range transmitters. I used Dad's serial number and authorization code, yes, his actual command code, to send a message straight to Commander Cramer.

So yeah. I committed a felony. A real one. Now I've written it down. Great job, Maria. No plausible deniability left. This diary entry can be used as evidence now.

I don't care. The message is encrypted. If Uncle John gets it, maybe... maybe... he can fix this.

We were supposed to lay low after that. Hide. Regroup. Let the grown-ups handle it. Yeah. That didn't happen. The Xaolin found us at the spaceport.

They didn't wait. Didn't hesitate. They opened fire the second they saw us. I don't know how long we ran, maybe five minutes, maybe five hours, but it felt like an eternity. Apparently, the "no collateral damage" clause in the assassin's code is more of a guideline.

We hid in luggage. No, seriously, we zipped ourselves into a duffel bag and tossed it into an inbound cargo crate. We prayed when it opened that it wouldn't be assassins with plasma blades. Secondary prayer that we didn't read wrong and end up in a cargo hold.

Instead? Civilians.

Who screamed like banshees when two teenagers tumbled out where their pajamas were supposed to be.

We bolted and disappeared into the nearby forest.

These are my woods. I grew up here. I know every cave, every broken tree, every place a person could vanish and never be found.

I led us to the only place I knew no one would follow: the family cemetery.

Who hides in a place where the only thing left to do after the murder is bury the body?

There's food, pear trees, shelter, and silence.

The groundskeeper was still there. Terida. Ancient. Eccentric. Somehow both sweet and unsettling.

Alley muttered, "You could dig a hole, stand her in it, and just add water." Not wrong.

She invited us in for fruit tea like we were long-lost cousins. She didn't blink when I gave a fake name, just nodded like she knew it already. When we left, she called me Mistress. For a moment, I thought she didn't remember who I was. She knew.

Before we left, she took me to Mr. Jenkave's grave. She said there was someone I needed to see. The people there were his family, paying their respects. I froze. Tried to run.

"Maria Roamai?" They stopped me.

I apologized... stammered something about the fire, about the accident, about how sorry I was.

I thought they would yell. Instead, they listened.

Alley tried to pull me away, but they hugged him... thanked him. They said they knew what he did to try and save Mr. Jenkave. The way I saw him deflate... like he had been carrying that guilt all along and I didn't even realize it.

They said they knew I tried too. That they couldn't face me then, but they could now.

They thanked my mom.

Apparently, she has been taking care of them this whole time... quietly, from a distance. She bought the house they live in. Set up a trust after the fire. Covered everything without saying a word. Of course she did. They tried to give me the patent back. I refused.

They offered to take us in. I told them it was too dangerous, that if the Xaolin found us it would put them at risk. They said it didn't matter. That we were family.

So here I am... laying on the floor of the house I thought I destroyed, rebuilt by the woman I thought I was becoming, and now owned by the people I thought would never forgive me.

I should feel guilty. I do. But I also feel... peace.

Just for tonight.

We'll leave in the morning. I don't know where we're going next, but for the first time in a long time... I don't feel like I'm running. Not yet.

Diary Entry # 60 – The Thin Line

A.T. 269, Month 5, Day 07 (Tulan Standard Time)

If I ever end up marrying someone, which, let's be honest, is so far down my priority list, it would be someone like Vaughn or Alley.

(Probably Alley. Okay... definitely Alley.)

We managed to get a message out to Vaughn today. He told us to stay put. Said he was ten minutes out. I didn't believe him until the knock at the door came ten literal minutes later... with a full division of 150 men.

He didn't even wait for us to explain. Before we could say a word, he played our own evidence back to us. Commander Cramer had received the message and broadcast it to all active operatives. The Executive General is now a fugitive.

I was elated. Then I was deflated. For a second, I thought it was over. That the worst part was done.

The army knows. He's exposed. That means the game's over, right?

Wrong.

He still has to be caught. Worse, he still has support. A surprising amount of it. Turns out an alliance between the Kameonic Army and the Xaolin isn't as unpopular as it should be.

Vault Diary - Hypothesis Oblivion

"Among the Chan," Vaughn said, "assassination is how you replace leadership. A tradition, not a tragedy." The horror of it hit me harder than I expected. Even now, with everything exposed, nothing is simple.

Vaughn gave me back my scanner. He said he had learned his lesson. Telling me to do nothing just guarantees I'll do it anyway. He deputized Alley as my official protector.

Deputy Protective Specialist. You've never seen anyone lean into a ridiculous title faster.

Vaughn was serious though. Comm reports every hour. Alley got assigned a drill sergeant who worked him half to death. (I think he loves it.)

We got barracks to ourselves, but Vaughn still dropped by after duty... late at night, hours after we were supposed to be asleep.

He told us stories. About deployments. About my dad. Said Dad took him in when he had nothing. Called him a brother, a mentor, a hero.

He said, "Your father saved my life. Not just from the Chan. He saved me from myself, from the ghosts that haunted me." He talked about Dad the way Alley talks about his own father. It hit me... Alley is to me what my dad is to Vaughn. A constant. A force I didn't know I needed until I had it. Until I might lose it.

When I first met Alley, I didn't get him. I thought he was loud, annoying, pushy. Reading those old entries now feels like spying on a stranger.

I miss that girl sometimes... the one who built models and thought she could insulate herself with science and structure. Who thought if she just stayed out of the world's way, it would leave her alone.

I wouldn't go back. She was strong in her way, but lonely. Scared. Pretending more than living.

Now? I'm still scared, but I know it. I don't pretend. I don't want to lose my moral center. Or my curiosity. Or what my parents call my "innocence." I don't want to go back to being safe, either.

Alley didn't give me a choice. He dragged me into this world of uncertainty and risk and real life. It wasn't always gentle. I didn't always like it.

Maybe that's exactly what I needed.

Vault Diary - Hypothesis Oblivion

Diary Entry # 61 – Shelter

A.T. 269, Month 5, Day 08 (Tulan Standard Time)

Short entry today. Nothing to report. Another boring day as an army intel intern.

The Xaolin transmissions are minimal. Repetitive, even. I swear I saw the exact same message twice... same words, same structure... sent at two completely different times.

I flagged it for Vaughn. He nodded like he'd expected it. Told me to take the rest of the day off.

I figured I'd write while the base is quiet. Alley's finishing morning drills.

I...

Diary Update:

Okay. So much for a short entry. I'll have to transcribe this later... assuming I live that long. The division was ambushed. Full-on ambushed. We're cut off. Reinforcements are five hours away. We won't last five hours. Vaughn's as confused as I am. Why now? Why send everything they've got at us?

I'm in a shelter now. I can hear blasts overhead. Every thud feels like it's aimed right at my spine. Alley's beside me. Tense. Focused. Arm cannon pointed at the front door. I've got mine pointed at the back. Finger on the trigger button. Holding still. Trying not to tremble.

I don't want to die. If you find this... Mom, Dad, Uncle Quince, Aunt Linda... I am so sorry for everything.

Alley just asked me if I could fire. If I had to. I told him I didn't think I could. I expected him to yell. To guilt me. To tell me I had to. He didn't. He told me to aim at the ceiling over the door.

I tried to ask him why but made the mistake of turning.

"EYES FRONT SOLDIER!"

I snapped back toward the door. We've been in silence ever since... eternal silence. Maybe the last peace of my life.

Alley did have an answer: "I won't berate you for not being willing to take a life. It's not a burden you should have to carry."

Mom, that is the answer I needed. Even if it cost me my life.

I asked if he could fire. He hasn't answered. The room is silent now... the kind that hurts, the kind that feels like a trap.

I hear footsteps...

no, above us...

BLAST

Vault Diary - Hypothesis Oblivion

Diary Entry # 62 – "No"

A.T. 269, Month 5, Day 08 (Tulan Standard Time)

This is not an update. I should never complain about quiet. The alternative is far worse.

I never got the chance to fire at the ceiling. According to Alley, both doors blew at once. The first one smashed into me. Knocked me flat. The Xaolin thought the blast killed me. It's the only reason I'm alive.

They didn't check. Didn't finish it. They were in a rush. Took Alley. Left me to burn.

When I came to, I was alone. No Alley. No soldiers. Just fire everywhere. The shelter was coming down around me. I stumbled out, driven by dread alone. The flames were a heartless taskmaster, ready to take my flesh as a toll for survival or my life for any wrong move.

I had to blast the door open and quickly turn around. Thank God they didn't take my shield arm cannon. The fire came pushing out once the doorway opened. Arm shield at max; it barely protected me... my arms blistering, screaming from heat.

Outside, the battle was still going. Alley was being dragged off, limp but alive.

I didn't think. I aimed down the sights of my shield arm cannon. I started blasting. Not at them — at the trees, the ground, the air around them. I wanted to miss. I didn't want to kill them. I wanted them to fire back. They did.

Three from one side. Two from another. Fortunately, the latter were too distracted to aim well. I held up my shield, took bolt after bolt.

The shield held... until it didn't. Too many blasts at once. The brace overheated — sparks, pressure, metal screaming.

I tore it off, threw it toward Alley's captors as close as I could get it, and ran.

The thing exploded mid-air, making a sizable crater in the clearing.

I don't remember hitting the wall after the blast. I woke up later... somewhere else.

Except... not really. I fell into a dream.

A nightmare. Worse than the battlefield.

I was surrounded. Enemies closing in. Alley was there, held by someone faceless. Waiting to die. Same question as always:
"Can you fire?"

This time... I didn't hesitate.
"No."

Vault Diary - Hypothesis Oblivion

I waited in dread for them to finish Alley off. I would be next. It wasn't the answer I wanted, but it was one I could die with.

The enemies dissolved instead. Alley smiled.

I don't know what it meant.

When I woke up, everything hurt less. Not physically. Emotionally. I'm in a hospital in Liviton now. Alley's beside me in a bed. Vaughn is sitting across the room, bandaged but alive.

He looked me in the eyes and said only this:
"You survived."

I'm writing this because I don't know how else to make sense of it. I'm not sure if putting this down makes me sane... or just confirms that I'm not. I'm here. So is Alley.

For now... that's enough.

Diary Entry # 63 – The General's Reckoning

A.T. 269, Month 5, Day 11 (Tulan Standard Time)

How could so much happen in two days?

I didn't write yesterday, not because I forgot or didn't have anything to say. I just didn't have the words. I didn't have the energy to pretend I was ready to think about it.

Now I do. Sort of.

Hospitals. I hate them.

I was hurt so badly that they couldn't use subdermal infusions. Too much tissue trauma, apparently. So… needles. Actual needles. Like something out of 40 PGC (Pre-Galactic Calendar). Alley called me a baby for flinching. Said it's not like they were stabbing me with a sword. I told him a sword would've been less insulting.

We were both resting, eyes closed, trading nonsense back and forth just to keep the silence at bay. The kind of calm you only find in hospitals, when everything hurts and nothing moves. We should have known something was wrong when the fire alarm went off. Our nurse assured us everything was fine, just a drill, then secured the door from the outside.

"They do those in top security hospitals? Leave the patients to die too, I bet. Part of protocol." We both giggled. If he knew how true that was, he wouldn't laugh. But we did. We laughed through his joke, through his follow-up. One more quip that I scarcely recall. I know it was a joke, but what stuck out was the stop. He stopped laughing. Stopped responding. Mid-sentence. Just... silence.

I opened my eyes and saw him.

Towelain.

He was there in a head medic's uniform. Standing over Alley's bed. No guards. No restraints. No announcement. He moved like a ghost, efficient, silent, hands already around Alley's neck and squeezing.

I screamed. Stumbled out of the bed and crashed into the nurse's station. The sound barely fazed him. He looked up, saw me, and crossed the room in three steps.

He backhanded me. No pretense, no posturing. Just power.

Everything inside me rattled... brain, vision, balance. I hit the floor like a Calbinite brick. He turned away from me, dismissed me without a second thought.

That was his only mistake.

I got up. Wobbled. My mouth tasted like copper and static. I stood anyway. He looked at me like I was an annoyance, like I was stupid for trying. I was getting in the way of what he really wanted to do. He wasn't wrong. He was four times my size, a war-bred lion. I was an ant, barely upright.

He came at me again, fast.

I moved first.

I ducked his swing, snatched the subdermal infuser off the nurse's tray, and jammed it against his side. Muscle relaxant. Triple the dose. No needle. Just pressure and chemistry.

He didn't even feel it at first. I didn't wait. I dove around him and yanked the cord off Alley's neck.

Alley gasped. One of those ragged, primal gasps... like drowning in reverse. I've never been so grateful to hear a cough in my life.

Towelain took one step toward us, then froze.

His arms twitched. His knees buckled as his body forgot how to move. He hit the floor like a slab of steel, his face slamming into a table on the way down.

When the nurse rushed in, I was already leaning over the comm and calling security. Told them what happened, who he was. Please hurry.

When Dad arrived, he didn't ask for details. He didn't need them.

He saw the bruise blooming on Alley's throat. The welt across my face. The Executive General on the ground. For a second, I thought I was going to have to testify against my own father at his murder trial.

He didn't kill Towelain. He didn't need to. The rogue general was paralyzed, already doomed.

The army brass was there before dawn. They took him away. Said he'd stand trial. He didn't.

Two nights later, someone broke into his holding cell. No effort to hide it. Just a body left slumped against the wall, and a Xaolin mark carved into the metal beside him.

Officially? Nothing to report.

Unofficially? Everyone knew. The army seized his assets. He no longer had the means to pay the Xaolin. Apparently, he thought he had assets beyond the reach of the army and promised to still pay Mistress Xao despite the seizures. He forgot my mother is an Inquisitor. What you hide, she will find.

He failed to get Carmen Foretto. I guess the prince did get the last laugh. With all his assets seized, both public and hidden, there was no way to pay them. The Xaolin Mistress didn't take too kindly to the bill remaining unpaid.

From the way Dad reported it, he might have had something to do with the army's "settlement" with the Xaolin. Either way, he assured us it was over.

After that... things finally got quiet.

Not silent. Not peaceful. Just still. No more sirens. No more running. No more knives in the dark.

Sometimes I still wake up expecting alarms, the sting of antiseptic in the air, the weight of someone's hand around my throat. The quiet at the farm feels wrong at first, like a trick I'm too tired to question. But then I hear the wind through the fields, the hum of machines instead of weapon fire, the sound of people breathing without fear. It isn't peace, not yet. It's something smaller, gentler—a world learning how to heal at the same pace I am.

Vault Diary - Hypothesis Oblivion

Diary Entry # 64 – Home

A.T. 269, Month 5, Day 34 (Tulan Standard Time)

Mom's finally back to her strict self, forcing me to diary again. After so long, I feel like I forgot how. After surviving so much, I figured living the now superseded writing about it. Besides, not reading about my nightmare of a life every night for a couple of weeks was a nice break. Don't worry, diary... I'll get you caught up. Where was I last?

Right after Towelain tried to kill us. I did mention he was removed. Thank God Dad didn't do it. Killed by his own assassins. I never wish anyone ill, but I'll admit I've slept better since I found out he was dead. I won't thank the Xaolin... just try to put it behind us. Pray the nightmares never return.

We were discharged the next morning.

All of us ended up back at the Maze family farm: me, Alley, Mom, Aunt Linda, Uncle Quince, and even Dad and Vaughn. Everyone stayed for two days. Just long enough to rest, to breathe, to not be hunted. It was less of a rest and more of a celebration, the opposite of a funeral, a festival of life. Music, dancing, laughter. I think it's the first party I ever enjoyed.

Aunt Linda stayed for two full weeks. She spoiled us the whole time. Army rations were replaced with real food. I'd forgotten how good things could taste when someone actually cared. She also, bless her, kept Mom from reclaiming full maternal dictatorship too soon, which was a minor miracle.

Mom has been different, though. Still sharp, still relentless, but softer. She didn't say much, but I could tell she's been watching me with a different lens.

On the last night of the party, Carmen Foretto arrived in full regalia, of course. Gold cape. Red boots. A collar that could stop solar flares. He swept into the house like a royal cyclone and kissed my hand like I was already famous.

"You saved my life," he said.

Mom blinked. Clearly, I had left that part out. He didn't ask how I was. He didn't ask what I needed. He brought an answer.

"With your permission," he said to Mom. He faltered when he noticed Dad. He bowed to my father, which earned him an indignant scowl. "With both of your permission, I'd like to build Maria a proper lab. On the farm. Fully stocked. A gift from the House of Foretto."

Uncle Quince raised an eyebrow. "I thought you gave up science."

I laughed. The first real one in a while.

Vault Diary - Hypothesis Oblivion

"No," I said. "I just stopped doing it wrong."

Mom nodded.

"It's already approved," she said. She insisted on one condition: voice access. For both of us.

She said it like it was a security measure, but I could hear the truth underneath. Trust. Not just in what I do, but in who I am.

Alley, of course, had to chime in: "Let's just hope she doesn't gas this one." *I am going to kill him.*

The lab's under construction now, right where the old storage shed used to be. They're keeping the outer frame, reinforcing it, but inside? All new.

Smart glass. Cold bays. Processors with more cores than I can count. Some tech I don't even recognize yet. The whole thing will be voice-activated. My voice.

Dad and Uncle Quince left yesterday evening, back to duty. They both said it like it was a joke I didn't get yet. Alley's still here. His dad's on another long haul, so he's staying with us a while. It's quiet tonight. That kind of quiet that doesn't feel fragile. Just... earned.

There's no cannon fire.
No sirens.
No assassins.

Just stars in the sky and the hum of something beginning again.

We'll never be the same. None of us. Maybe we're not supposed to be.

This isn't a happy ending. It's just the first one we got to choose.

Tomorrow? I'll build something.
Because I want to.
Because I know how.
Because I'm still here.

For the first time in a long time... I'm not waiting for the sky to fall.